Jake caught sight of Cass sailing past them.

How she'd managed to survive all these hours, he'd never know. But that was Cass.

Tough.

Stubborn.

Determined.

Amazing.

He stood rooted to the spot, letting Max sniff to his heart's content while he drank in the sight of her. The neat blazer she wore was now rumpled and no doubt stained from her attempts to stay fed and hydrated. Though her golden-brown hair flew loose around her face, he remembered the way she'd struggled to pull a comb through it after riding with the car window rolled down. Jake had no doubt it would be a tangle of snarls when she got off the ride.

And they would get her off there.

DANGER
ON THE MIDWAY

MAGGIE WELLS

INTRIGUE

Dedicated to all of our four-legged protectors—
professional and domestic. Particularly Timber—
our ever faithful, always vigilant, much beloved fluffer nutter.

Recycling programs
for this product may
not exist in your area.

ISBN-13: 978-1-335-69076-0

Danger on the Midway

Harlequin Enterprises ULC
22 Adelaide St. West, 41st Floor
Toronto, Ontario M5H 4E3, Canada
www.Harlequin.com

HarperCollins Publishers
Macken House, 39/40 Mayor Street Upper,
Dublin 1, D01 C9W8, Ireland
www.HarperCollins.com

Printed in Lithuania

1 2 3 4 5 6 7 8 9 10 LIT 28 27 26 25

By day, **Maggie Wells** is buried in spreadsheets. At night, she pens tales of intrigue and people tangling up the sheets. She has a weakness for hot heroes and happy endings. She is the product of a charming rogue and a shameless flirt, and you only have to scratch the surface of this mild-mannered married lady to find a naughty streak a mile wide.

Books by Maggie Wells

Harlequin Intrigue

Arkansas Special Agents

Ozarks Missing Person
Ozarks Double Homicide
Ozarks Witness Protection
Danger on the Midway

Arkansas Special Agents: Cyber Crime Division

Shadowing Her Stalker
Catching a Hacker
Ozarks Conspiracy

A Raising the Bar Brief

An Absence of Motive
For the Defense
Trial in the Backwoods

Foothills Field Search

Visit the Author Profile page at Harlequin.com.

CAST OF CHARACTERS

Captain Jake Donovan—Arkansas State Police Special Agent K-9 Division. Jake and his partner, Max, are charged with sniffing out multiple explosive devices. He's also Cassidy Walker's high school sweetheart.

Trooper Max—A hyper-vigilant German shepherd trained to be a canine detection agent. He specializes in identifying the presence of explosives and narcotics.

Cassidy Walker—Head of Security for the Arkansas State Fair. A former US Air Force Security Service Specialist, Cassidy is being held hostage by a bomber who seems to have a vendetta against her.

Colonel Steve Aronson—Arkansas State Police tactical response unit. Appointed site commander for joint state and municipal forces working the investigation.

Bud Thompson—Retired Little Rock Police investigator working for Fair security. Cassidy's right hand man.

Sergeant Evan Furst—Lead bomb disposal technician for the Little Rock Fire Department.

Chapter One

Cassidy Walker was having a good morning. A surprisingly good morning.

The alarm went off with enough time to grab a coffee and a sausage biscuit on her way in to work. She hadn't spilled any of her breakfast on her top. Her hair was cooperating. And so was the weather. For the past few years, the Arkansas State Fair had been mostly rained out.

Not this year.

Tipping her head back, she checked the bright blue October sky. Nope. Not a single cloud. The forecast for the next ten days showed clear skies and pleasantly cool temperatures.

So, yes. Things had been going exceptionally well for the day before the opening of the fair. The weeks leading up to this day had been a scramble. Media Day was usually a complete circus, too, but here they were. Everything that could be done was done.

Their PR team had sent passes to news outlets all around the state. The food vendors had spent hours prepping for the VIP tasting scheduled for early afternoon. Arcade barkers had decorated their booths with tempting plush animals. The ride operators, having completed final run-throughs, had provided good b-roll for the news cameras.

So far, so good. Cassidy couldn't help but feel optimistic as she hung back, allowing the group of elementary school children who'd earned a morning at the fair with perfect attendance to scurry to get close to the man leading the way to the fair's carnival midway—Governor James Henry Beauford.

The kids were props for a photo opportunity with the governor. And for once, the big man was running on schedule. Maybe even a little early. Shocking for a politician known for stopping and chatting with anybody who dared to make direct eye contact.

He smiled and chatted with the children as they lined up to pose in front of the gilt-painted carousel. He flashed his spotlight of a smile at each child, knowing the cameras captured every moment. The snowy-haired gentleman charmed both the schoolchildren and the media.

"Born to glad-hand."

The man beside her chuckled. Special Agent Ryan Hastings from the Arkansas State Police led the governor's personal protection detail. They'd met the previous day at a security briefing, and Cassidy had liked the man right away. He didn't have any of the overinflated self-importance she'd come to expect from many of the men in his position.

"This is all for nothing," he said. "They're not even old enough to vote."

"Can we get some shots of the governor and the kids on the carousel?" the media director shouted over the high-pitched music.

Hastings groaned as the children cheered and Beauford gave his own hearty cheer of approval.

Cassidy shot a pitying glance at the harried teacher who'd been charged with shepherding the group of overstimulated first graders through the morning's schedule. "You get your guy, I'll help herd the little ones," she said to the special agent. "The sooner we do this, the quicker it's over."

They managed to get everyone on the merry-go-round with surprisingly little fuss. One boy, a skinny little slip of a kid with huge eyes and an even bigger backpack strapped to his back, opted to sit on one of the ride's stationary benches. The hairs on her arms rose.

She eyed the bag with a puzzled frown. It was well over the limit they imposed on bags at the entry points. Reaching for the two-way radio clipped to her belt, she said, "Stanford, you read me?"

The man who oversaw the security checkpoint at the south gate answered right away. "Copy."

"Y'all are checking bags, aren't you?"

"Ten-four."

"I'm seeing some that shouldn't have gotten by."

There was a pause. "Yes, ma'am. Of course, there's a lot of camera and audio equipment coming in today." Static crackled. "I'll make sure we tighten it up."

"Ten-four."

Cassidy winced as the operator also cranked up the canned calliope music. The same syrupy-sweet tunes would play in her sleep for weeks after the fair ended. Grimacing, she grasped the pole closest to her. Why couldn't her brain latch on to the thrash metal they blasted at some of the scarier rides?

As the carousel picked up speed, she clung to a nearby horse. The scent of oil and sugar carried on the breeze. Her stomach flipped even as her mouth watered. Cassidy sighed. She was prepared for the next ten days. The hunger for junk food edging out nervous nausea. The scents of hay and animals from the barns. The temptations of the concessions offering everything from fresh-squeezed lemonade to deep-fried butter. She was unashamedly partial to those huge smoked-turkey legs.

A glance over her shoulder told her the governor was in his element. Standing beside a blonde girl riding a white horse with a glittering gold mane and tail, she watched a boy stand up in the stirrups of his trusty gray steed and give a whoop of excitement. A grandfather of eight, Beauford threw his head back and laughed heartily.

The footage would play beautifully on the evening news.

Smiling, she turned her attention to the midway as they whirled past. Media Day was a busy one, but nowhere near as chaotic as Opening Day. She should enjoy this relative calm before the storm.

But she couldn't wait for it all to get started.

The weeks leading up to the fair were a grind of endless meetings and walk-throughs. Once the gates opened to the public, the action kicked into high gear. Parking-lot fender benders. The constant competition and sometimes outright sabotage between vendors. Fights breaking out in the lines for the carnival rides. Tearful reunions between frightened parents and their wandering kids. The neon lights. The obnoxious cajoling and taunts of the barkers running the games.

These ten days encapsulated the kind of mostly harmless bedlam she thrived on.

Instinctively, she checked the sky again. Still no sign of rain clouds. This year would be different. Exhaling long and soft, she allowed her shoulders to relax. There'd be no torrential storms dampening attendance numbers and setting tempers on edge. Conditions looked to be optimal.

The grounds should be crowded during the day. On the weekdays, office workers would come for lunch and teenagers would rule the nights. The weekends would be packed with families.

It was a good day, and if her luck held, it would be an even better week.

Cassidy's phone vibrated in her jacket pocket. She pulled it out and saw a text from an unknown caller. Not unusual. Nearly every exhibitor, vendor and fair worker had her mobile number. Still, if anyone truly needed her, they'd call over the radio.

"Should we go again?"

The governor's suggestion was met by the cheers of the children. Between them and her exaggerated groan, they almost managed to drown out the familiar calliope music blaring from hidden speakers.

There were ten thousand other tasks she should be handling. But she couldn't bail with the governor on the ride. Not for anything short of an emergency. Gripping the pole tighter with one hand, she pulled her radio from her belt with the other. She needed to check to be sure things were good to go for the rest of the day's events.

Pressing the button, she raised it close to her lips. "Bud, you read me?"

A moment passed before her second-in-command answered her call. "Thompson here."

She turned away from the other adults on the ride and spoke quietly. "Hey, the big guy is having a good time down here. Looks like we're going around again. Everything good up there?"

"We're set up for the tasting. A few media types have wandered up here. I think they're afraid they'll miss out on the…" he paused for dramatic effect "…Cream-filled, Strawberry-dipped, Deep-fried, Chocolate-drizzled Funnel Cake on a Stick."

"Holy cow," she said with a chuckle.

"Nope, I think the cow would be the BBQ Bacon Pineapple Cheeseburger."

Cassidy smiled. Bud Thompson's affinity for fair food oddities was a running joke between them. "Well, you've got a good thirty minutes before they set up. Someone checking to be sure everything is under control in RV city?"

"Ten-four, boss."

Smirking, she hooked her radio on her waistband. She cast a glance at the livestock barns as they spun past. The first rounds of judging had started the previous weekend. Many of the exhibitors camped within the fairgrounds so they could care for their animals while in competition. It wasn't unusual for there to be territorial disputes between families, and while the temps they hired for security were enthusiastic, they lacked Bud's experience in deescalating tense situations.

Resolved to enjoy this moment of peace, she closed her eyes and focused on the feel of the warm breeze on her face. She refused to think about what the constant swirl was doing to her once-cooperative hair.

Her phone buzzed again.

She reached into her blazer pocket and pulled out the device. Sure enough, missed messages from unknown numbers were stacking up. Sighing, she opened the app to the green bubble of an SMS message.

Do not stop the ride.

What the hell... She looked up and down the midway. Aside from the merry-go-round, only a handful of carnival rides were active.

A moment later, a second message appeared.

Do not get off the ride.

Her heart dropped into her stomach as she reread those chilling words, and her grip tightened as she stepped closer to the edge of the platform, scanning the area as she turned.

She scrolled back to the first of the messages.

Hang on tight. I have a surprise for you.

Her mind racing, she thumbed through the rest of the texts she'd put off reading. One from a food vendor looking for a lost delivery, another from the woman who was overseeing one of the arts and crafts competitions. Then there was one that made her breath catch in her throat.

I've planted explosive devices throughout the fairgrounds.

"Oh no," she exhaled. "No. No. No-no-no," she said as she started weaving her way through the galloping horses, her eyes fixed on the man standing a few feet away from the governor.

"Hastings." She raised a hand to hail the tall man as she approached.

He looked up with a smirky smile, but it quickly melted away. He straightened and closed the gap between them in two strides. "What is it?"

Not wanting to cause any panic, she thrust her phone out for him to see. The moment he digested the gist of the threat, he barked, "Stop the ride," and turned in the direction of the governor.

"No!" Digging her heels in, she pulled him back. "We can't stop. Look."

Do not stop the ride.

Do not get off the ride.

"Yeah, well, no," he said. "My duty is to my principal, and we're getting off this thing."

"But what if it's on here?"

"I have to get him out of the area," he said, grinding out each word. "We'll slow it down and jump off."

"They told us not to get off," she argued, following as he strode in the opposite direction of the ride's movement.

He stopped in his tracks, his expression softening apologetically but his jaw taut with determination. "Whoever this is told *you* not to get off the ride," he pointed out quietly.

Cassidy gaped at his back. She stared in disbelief as the operator leaped onto the deck with practiced ease, talked to Special Agent Hastings, then jumped off a moment later. Within seconds, the carousel slowed.

By the time it wound down to a creep, full-blown panic crawled up her throat. The only word she could force past the lump lodged there was, "No!"

Hastings held on to Governor Beauford's arm as he shot a glance at her. "We're having a mechanical issue," the governor announced, raising his voice to be heard over the incessant music. "We can't stop the ride, so we're going to have to hop off."

Hastings must have radioed for backup, because two state troopers in uniform appeared as if conjured. They steadied the governor as he jumped from the platform, his politician's smile never slipping. "This is why we test run these things." He waved encouragingly to the gaggle of press. "Hey, kids, you want to go check out the cows?"

The small crowd around the carousel quickly fell into step behind the jovial politician. Cassidy pulled her phone from her pocket again and typed out a reply.

Who are you? Why are you doing this?

The three dots danced at the bottom of her screen. A response came through with periods emphasizing each word.

Do. Not. Stop. The. Ride.

She looked up, a grim frown tugging at her lips. She caught sight of the skinny young man at the operator's controls. The next time she passed him, she said, "Can you kill the music?"

He tugged his ball cap lower on his forehead. "Are we done here?"

"I'm not, but you are. Don't stop the ride, but cut the calliope, and grab one of the officers for me."

Firing off the first questions that came to mind, she typed furiously.

Who are you? What do you want?

She waited, her throat dry, praying she'd get something, anything, more out of whoever was doing this.

Another number popped up seconds later, but the message read simply, Twelve.

"Twelve? Twelve what? Twelve o'clock? Twelve bombs?"

Cassidy typed frantically, copying and pasting her queries into each of the text threads in a desperate attempt to maintain contact.

But no one replied.

Pulling the radio from her waistband, she held it to her mouth. "All available security personnel to the…" She paused as she tried to catch sight of a good spot for an outpost nearby but not too close. "Report to the central midway—Manny's corn dog stand," she ordered. "Quickly."

She was struggling to clip it to her belt with trembling hands when a man in turnout pants came trotting up to the operator's station.

"Ma'am?"

"If you want to talk to me, you have to come aboard." She closed her eyes against a rising wave of nausea.

She heard the thud of heavy boots hitting the metal platform and forced herself to look in their direction. The firefighter approached. His expression of grim determination spoke volumes.

"You know what's happening?"

"Sergeant Evan Furst, Little Rock Fire Department Tactical Response Squad." He introduced himself. "Special Agent Hastings gave me the gist."

Cassidy's years in military, security and law-enforcement-adjacent careers helped her recognize the double speak used for "bomb squad" when she heard it.

"We've got a real situation here, Sarge," she said with a wan smile.

Gesturing to something behind her, he looked worried. "There's a bench seat, ma'am. Why don't you sit down? Try to focus on something stationary."

"Do I look bad?" She gave a shaky laugh.

"I'm only saying we've got a real situation here, ma'am," he said, tossing her words back at her in a deceptively light tone. "Special Agent Hastings has alerted Arkansas State Police Headquarters. They're sending specialists. There's a bomb threat?"

"Yes. They replied with the number twelve, but I don't know if means twelve o'clock or twelve bombs," she confirmed. "The initial message said 'devices' plural, though, so let's assume more than one."

"Yes, ma'am."

"I've asked my security team to assemble at the corn dog stand." She gestured vaguely at the asphalt midway.

"We're on it, ma'am. Are you in radio communication with your team?"

"Yes," she said, fighting down the bile rising in her throat.

"Good. I will liaise with them and with the other tactical teams as they assemble. If you'd relay all the messages sent via radio once I get with your team, I'd appreciate it. We want to keep the suspect's line of communication as uncluttered as possible."

"Will do." A knot of dread tightened in her stomach as she watched him hop down from the ride. Before he made it more than three strides, she called out to him. "I could use some water."

Sergeant Furst raised a hand to let her know he'd heard her, moved two of the metal crowd-control panels to close off access to the operator's station, then trotted off in the direction of the food stands in the center of the carnival.

Cassidy forced herself to put her phone in her blazer pocket, then, swinging from pole to pole, made her way to a gaudily painted bench bookended by sparkly green seahorses. She kept her eyes trained on her feet, trying to block out the motion by focusing on the tips of her lug-soled boots.

Sliding into the double bench, she dropped down heavily on the wooden seat, wondering idly who would ever choose to ride a merry-go-round seated backward.

A soft shuffling sound to her right made her freeze. Tearing her gaze from the tips of her shoes, she turned to find the small, skinny kid with the enormous backpack staring up at her wide-eyed.

"Did you say there's a bomb?"

Chapter Two

"What have we got?" Captain Jake Donovan slid from the driver's seat of his state-issued SUV. Squinting into the late-morning sun, he raised a hand to shade his eyes before reaching for a black cap with the Arkansas State Police logo.

"Bomb threat." The firefighter hooked a thumb over his shoulder, then offered his hand. "Sergeant Evan Furst. I'm lead technician with the LRFD bomb squad."

He shook hands with the young man in the LRFD shirt who'd met him at the south gate in an ATV, intent on taking Jake straight down onto the fairground's colorful carnival midway.

"Where are we at?" Jake walked around to the passenger side of his vehicle before pressing the button on his key fob to release the rear door. He gave a short, sharp whistle and Max, a ninety-pound German shepherd, jumped out of the vehicle and promptly sat at Jake's feet.

"We're assembled near the corn dog stand, but Colonel Aronson is in the arena at the moment." Furst gestured toward the midway.

"Let's head down there first, then I'll check in with the boss." He jerked his chin in the direction of the carnival rides. "What have we got?"

Furst nodded. "We believe there's at least one device on the merry-go-round."

Beyond the food stand, the garishly outfitted carousel spun in a slow circle. Jake frowned as he noted it was the only ride in motion. The only one with people on it. But there was no music playing. The entire carnival was oddly quiet.

"It's on there? Why is it running?"

"Instructions from head of Security, sir," Furst explained with a grimace. "The threat came through to her via text message. Whoever is doing this said not to stop the carousel."

"Text message?" Jake turned his head sharply, his brow furrowed in confusion. "And we think the device is on the ride?"

Sergeant Furst's lips thinned into a tight line as he nodded. "The informant gave specific instruction not to the stop the ride. They claim there are multiple devices scattered around the grounds."

"Do we know how many?"

"Head of Security is guessing twelve, but we are not certain."

"Twelve?"

His tone was sharp enough to elicit a head tilt and a grunt from Max. Without looking, he reached down and placed a hand on his K-9 partner's head to reassure the dog. Max sometimes had a better read on his emotions than he did himself.

He bent to be sure Max's lead was securely clipped to his harness. The breakaway feature of the leash allowed him to deploy Max when they needed his speed and agility, but there were too many people around, and Jake didn't have a clear picture on where they should begin their search.

"Who are all these people? I didn't think the fair opened until tomorrow."

"Media Day." They set off in the direction of the corn dog stand. "There are also workers finishing setup." An autumnal breeze carried the scent of smoked meats and cooking grease. "Food prep, too, I imagine," Furst added with a wry smirk. "They were taking photos with the governor and some kids from one of the local schools when Security called us in."

"The governor's here?" Jake's eyes widened.

"Safe. His personal detail got him off the ride and into Barton." Furst pointed toward the old arena in the center of the fairgrounds.

"And there was no detonation?" Jake asked.

"No, sir. We're not sure what might trigger one, though," Furst admitted.

Once the premier entertainment venue in Central Arkansas, Barton Coliseum lost its headliners to newer, flashier arenas, but still served as home to rodeos, monster truck rallies and other regional events.

Jake looked around. "And where is this 'head of Security'…?" he prompted, letting the question dangle.

"Walker," Furst advised.

Jake's steps slowed as he caught sight of a blonde woman on one of the carousel benches, holding hands with a gangly boy seated across from her. The fanciful seahorses on the ends of the seats sported glittering blue-green paint. The boy sat on the edge of his seat, a black backpack looped over his narrow shoulders.

"Why is there a kid on there?" But before he could pick up the pace again, the woman moved to sit on the same bench as the boy. They hugged, then seemed to tussle a bit. "What the—" Jake clicked his tongue once and took off in a flat run. "Hey, lady! Miss!" He sprinted toward the carousel. "Ma'am! Stop!"

Max galloped easily beside him, insultingly unwinded and enjoying the uphill jaunt.

"Ma'am," Jake tried again, but he was too late.

Somehow the woman had managed to loop her arm through one of the backpack straps as the boy slithered loose. Now her young friend stood at the end of the bench and the black straps were settled firmly on her shoulders.

"Somebody grab him," she shouted as they spun past again.

The wind caught the little boy's oversize orange T-shirt as he stared at the ground swirling past the edge of the platform, his hand wrapped tightly around one of the poles supporting the canopy.

Using his nephews as a gauge, Jake guessed the kid was no more than six or seven. Tears ran down the boy's face as he inched closer to the edge. Jake heard the woman call out again, shouting for someone to help the boy down.

They pulled up inside the metal fencing around the ride. Unfurling some slack in Max's lead, he gave the dog the command to stay and then stepped forward. "I've got you, buddy." He reached out to the boy the next time he passed. "You can meet my dog."

The ride made another circuit, but this time Jake could see the kid wanted off but was scared to make the leap. All long, gangly arms and knobby knees, the boy braced to jump. "You'll catch me?"

"Absolutely," Jake shouted after him.

When he came around again, Jake counted down in a firm, commanding tone. "Three, two, one, jump!"

Max added emphasis to the prompt with a short, sharp bark.

The boy flung himself at Jake, who stumbled back on impact. The kid's skinny limbs wrapped around him, and he hung on like a koala clinging to a tree trunk.

He wrapped the boy up tightly. "There you go, little man," Jake said, breathless. "Good jump."

"I was scared," the small boy said, speaking into the crook of Jake's neck.

"I know, but you did good."

The boy peeled himself away enough to frown down at the bulky tactical vest Jake wore. "You're all lumpy."

Chuckling, Jake nodded as he turned away from the ride, determined to make the promised introduction then hand the boy off as soon as possible. "I guess I am. Wanna meet Max?"

Lowering the boy to the tarmac, he set him down beside the dog outfitted in matching tactical harness. Sitting at attention, they were almost the same height, but a good portion of his stature could be attributed to the dog's ears.

"Trooper Max, meet… Hey, what's your name?"

"Darien." The boy stared back at him with eyes almost as big as Max's ears. "He's big. Does he bite?"

"Nah, never the good guys," Jake said, giving Max's head a gentle stroke to let the dog know all was well.

Darien mimicked the move, then instantly stepped back. "I never petted a big dog before," he confessed. Then, as though he feared he'd insulted Max, he quickly added, "He's real soft though."

"Yes. Very soft."

Furst reappeared with a woman wearing a T-shirt that matched Darien's. After identifying her as his teacher, Jake flashed her a quick smile in response to the profusion of thanks and admonishments flowing from the woman's lips. He patted Darien's back and gave him a gentle shove into the woman's grasping hands. "Go on, buddy. Max and I have work to do."

Straightening, he watched her lead her young charge away before turning to the firefighter. "Where's this Walker person?" he demanded, switching gears without missing a beat.

Sergeant Furst nodded to the ride as the blonde wearing the backpack came whirling past again. "There."

"She's the head of Security?" Jake caught a glimpse of wispy blond hair she disappeared around the other side again.

"Cassidy Walker," Furst affirmed. He glanced down at a small notebook. "Been working for the state fair for nearly three years. Former training officer for US Air Force Security Forces, 19th Security Forces Squadron, Little Rock AFB."

"Cassidy Walker." Jake's mind reeled as if he was the one stuck on a merry-go-round.

"Excuse me," the woman on the carousel called as she swung past them again.

Both men looked up in time to see her hold her mobile phone

high. But they waited until she came around again to catch what she was shouting at them.

"He's watching." She waved the phone again. "They saw—"

Jake waited a beat then gave his partner the signal to come to heel. "Who saw what?"

"—saw me take the backpack," she shouted on her next pass.

She spun around to the other side again and he stepped closer. "Come on, Max."

The dog didn't have to be told twice. Quickly taking up the slack in his lead, he leaped agilely onto the slow-moving ride. Jake had no choice but to follow, since his partner was clearly onto the scent of something at the base of one of the stationary horses.

He allowed the dog a moment to sniff his fill, then retracted some of the leash. "Whatcha got, boy? Something good?" Max looked up, his amber eyes bright with excitement. "Good boy. Come on, let's see what's happening here."

Gripping poles as they walked against the movement of the ride, he kept his eyes fixed on the woman seated in the seahorse seat. Her back was to him. Stands of streaky dark blond hair flew into her face. He watched as she batted them away impatiently. Her head swiveled as they came around to the midway side again. He caught her frown in profile, then spoke softly, not keen to startle the woman who may or may not have willingly strapped a bomb onto her back.

She wouldn't be the first possible terrorist to work from the inside.

But Cassidy Walker wasn't a terrorist. At least, the Cassidy Walker he'd once known wasn't. She'd been the most upright, no-nonsense woman he'd ever met. Stubborn, too. And brave.

Brave enough to keep wriggling her way into holding an incendiary device so everyone around her could go free.

"Hey, Cass," he said, coming to a stop a few inches behind

the bench. He ignored Max's warning whine but could feel
the dog beside him tense with anticipation. "Remember me?"

Everything inside Cassidy stilled at the sound of his voice. She
wet her dry lips and lowered her chin to her chest, her mind
racing as she tried to come to grips with her circumstances.

Her hair blew into her eyes. She swept it away, thinking
about how smug she'd felt about everything earlier. The good
hair day. A picture-perfect October sky.

The bombs planted around her fairgrounds.

How had it all gone so wrong?

"Cass?"

He called her name again. He was here. The man calling to
her was not a figment of her overwrought imagination. He was
as real as the backpack she'd willingly strapped to her back.
Screwing her eyes shut, she wondered if maybe she was dead.

Maybe the jerk who'd sent those text messages had detonated a bomb.

Someone touched her shoulder, but she didn't turn to look.
She didn't need to. She wasn't dead and this wasn't all some
kind of daytime nightmare. It was actually happening.

"Jake." She croaked his name. It was neither greeting nor
warning. Simply a whisper carried off on one of the endless
circuits.

"Cass, what is happening?"

"My day isn't going as planned."

She tried to inject her words with a light, mocking tone,
but it fell short. No matter. She focused on keeping her eyes
fixed on the chipping green paint on the bench across from her.
After more than a half hour whirling in circles, she'd given up
on looking at anything more than a couple feet in front of her.

"I saw you take that backpack." The statement contained a
gentle chide. She felt a surge of hot indignation spark deep in

her belly, but she shut it down. Losing control could mean disaster. She swallowed hard then spoke in a slow, measured tone.

"Well, I wasn't going to leave Darien holding the bag." She eyed him warily. "What brings you here?"

Sensing a movement to her right, she blinked slowly. When she opened her eyes, she was shocked to find a pair of amber ones staring back at her rather than Jake's sea-blues.

The dog's nose twitched and then he bared his teeth with a growl. But there was no menace in the tone. It was simply a warning. Was he warning her? Or warning Jake about her?

"Oh. Hi…" she blurted.

"Max," Jake disclosed, stepping into her line of vision behind the dog.

He murmured something in a soothing tone and the dog settled onto its haunches, a soft wuffling noise escaping with each impatient exhale.

"Hey, Max," she said in a trembling voice.

"He's not a fan of your new backpack," Jake said in a quiet, confidential tone. He sat on the bench directly across from her. "What were you thinking, Cass?"

"Cassidy." The correction was automatic. No one called her Cass anymore. Only Jake Donovan had ever called her Cass. "And I figured better me than a seven-year-old boy."

"Noble," he said, lifting a single eyebrow.

The familiarity of look both comforted her and set her blood simmering. "Yep. I'm the queen of self-sacrifice," she shot back, her tone drenched in sarcasm. She took in his tactical gear and the vest on the dog seated between them. "I see you got your dream job."

He didn't ask her to clarify. There was no need. Jake's sights had been firmly set on joining the Arkansas State Police since one of the troopers who lived in their town had made an appearance at the seventh-grade career fair.

"This isn't how I pictured running into you again," he said

with a wry twist of a smile. His gaze dropped and he nodded to her lap. "Is the phone you received the messages on?"

Jerking slightly at the change in topic, she looked down to where she practically strangled the device she held with both hands. A hot blush crept up her neck. Of course he wanted to see the phone. He hadn't come here looking for her. "Oh. Yeah. Yes."

He leaned in closer and extended his hand. "May I?"

She thrust the phone at him. "Here."

He took it from her. "Do you know how Darien got the backpack?"

"He said a guy gave it to him at one of the midway games. Told him there was a game console in there, but he shouldn't open it or the big kids would take it away."

Jake grunted, then frowned at the phone screen. "Security code?"

"It's 888927," she recited.

This time, both eyebrows flew up. The heat in her cheeks intensified as she realized he recognized the repurposing of her parents' old phone number.

"My mom told me your folks moved to Florida," he said as he keyed in the sequence. The one he'd once kept programmed in his own phone.

"They did," she confirmed.

"They like it down there?" He scanned the text bubbles. Each message came through to her phone from a different unknown contact.

"Jake, I don't think this is a great time for a catch-up," she said, her voice taut with tension.

He blew out a breath. "SMS messages. I don't suppose you recognize any of the incoming phone numbers."

She shook her head. "I figure they're using a random number generator. I've been forwarding them to the guy in charge… Something Anson."

"Aronson," he said, supplying the name of the SWAT commander who'd summoned all available detection agents to the scene. "Colonel Aronson."

Cassidy resisted the urge to roll her eyes like she would have when they were young. "Sorry. I was too busy trying to keep the governor, a gaggle of media types and a classroom of kids from getting blown sky-high to get all the details."

"Gotcha." He scanned the messages. "And the last one said…"

She nodded toward the device. "The top number. Something about being brave or stupid." She played it off with a nonchalant wave of her hand, but she remembered the text word for word.

I don't know if you're incredibly brave or truly stupid, Lieutenant Walker.

Jake looked up, a furrow of concern digging a trench between his eyes. "Lieutenant Walker?"

"Second Lieutenant, US Air Force," she intoned through numb lips.

"This is someone who knows you," Jake concluded.

It wasn't an accusation. She knew it wasn't. Still, it felt like one. "Or knows of me," she retorted stiffly. "My service record is mentioned in my public bio."

"Where could someone find that bio?"

She shrugged. "It's on the fair website. Social media." She tried to shrug, but suddenly the pack on her back seemed to weigh a thousand pounds. "They hired me because they liked my military experience. Used to be based at Little Rock Air Force Base."

"I see." He looked back down at her phone. "Not giving us a lot of detail, are they?"

She shook her head then glanced at her watch. It was almost noon. The food vendors expected to provide samples for the press. Her second-in-command, a retired Little Rock police corporal named Bud Thompson, had said a handful of them hadn't been terribly cooperative when he'd instructed everyone to go to the arena while they assessed the threat.

"Have you looked in there?" Jake tilted his head to glance meaningfully at the backpack.

Pressing her lips together, Cassidy could only shake her head. "Afraid to move it too much."

"What does it feel like?"

She closed her eyes and concentrated on the weight pulling on her shoulders. "Hard casing. Probably plastic, judging by the weight. Five pounds, maybe? No more than ten," she concluded, opening her eyes again.

"No sounds? No heat? No vibrations?"

She shook her head. "No." She let out a huff of a laugh. "Feels like a gaming console," she said with a wry smile. "Do you think I ripped poor Darien off?"

He met her attempt at levity with a somber stare. "No. But I'm going to let Max give you a sniff. Okay?"

She nodded and he snapped his fingers. The large dog bounded up beside her on the bench as if he thought they'd never ask. Cassidy tried not to flinch as his cool nose brushed the side of her neck. He whined and growled softly, the sound practically vibrating inside her. She winced and shied away when the dog gave three sharp barks in quick succession then dropped onto the bench.

"He's trained in explosives, huh?" She grimaced at the sad attempt at small talk but was unable to come up with anything better under the circumstances.

He gave two quick snaps of his fingers, and Max hopped down, resuming his position at Jake's feet. She watched as he gave the dog a head scratch, murmured a word of praise and pulled a small treat out of his pocket.

"He's done a bit of search and rescue when needed but specializes in detection. Explosives and narcotics."

"And?" she prompted, hating the quaver in her voice.

"It's explosives. Likely an IED," he confirmed.

She shot Max a nervous glance. "How do you know it's not weed or something?"

Jake gave the dog another pat. "He gives different signals to let me know what's detected. That way, I know how to approach."

"Right. Makes sense." She nodded like a bobblehead, anxious to make it clear she wasn't entirely without expertise in this area.

"I think I should hold on to this," he said, holding her phone up. "You know cell signals can interfere with whatever kind of transmitter they're using."

"Right."

"You have a radio?"

She nodded and moved to unclip it from her waistband, but he stopped her. "Keep it. They work on a different kind of bandwidth, low frequency." He glanced over his shoulder. "Got any extras around?"

She raised the radio. "Thompson?"

A second later, a gruff voice came across. "Copy, Chief."

"Would you grab one of the extra radios for Trooper Donovan to use?"

Bud's response was a curt, "Will do."

Her phone buzzed in his hand, and they both looked down. Another text.

Jake opened a new message from yet another unknown number.

Give her the phone back.

"I told you they can see us," she said, snatching the device from his hand. She and Jake both craned their necks, scoping the entire area for anyone close enough to see them sitting knee to knee.

"Must be a camera around," he concluded.

"Probably more than one. Security has cameras and the company who manages the rides and attractions have some of their own, but these rides are dismantled and rebuilt a lot. Not sure how many there are or what condition they might be in."

Jake hazarded a guess. "They could be hacking into them."

"Or whoever it is planted a few more. No one would have noticed," she said, glaring down at her phone. She tapped on the reply box and began typing.

"What are you doing?"

"We need to know what these people want." Biting her lip, she tapped out a message.

What do you want? How do we stop this?

She showed the display to Jake, then shifted on the bench, trying to get comfortable without leaning back against the weighty pack. Gnawing her bottom lip, she gripped the phone tighter, willing the person on the other end to answer. Long minutes passed before Jake rose. When the message came through, it made her blood run cold.

I have a dozen reasons. Cooperate.

"Jake," she said, her voice a little shakier than she'd like.

But he was already moving to leave. "I'm sending someone down to stay nearby while I talk to Aronson and find out what the plan—"

Whatever he was going to say next was lost in the void following a shattering explosion. Jake dropped to one knee in front of her, but Max stood his ground. Cassidy twisted on the bench, hindered by the bulk of the backpack as she cast about, trying to ascertain the location of the explosion.

Booted feet pounded the pavement. She caught sight of a group of firefighters beating a path toward the north gate. Her radio crackled to life. Bud Thompson's voice came across, brusque and breathless. "North ticket booth blown to smithereens."

She grabbed at her handset, nearly ripping the belt loop from her pants in her haste. "Is the area secured? Casualties?"

"Negative," came the gruff, disembodied voice. "On our way."

"Stay put," Jake commanded, snapping her attention to him.

She glared at him. "I'm getting tired of people telling me to stay on this stupid ride."

"Do it anyway," he ordered. "We don't know what this person's plan or goal is. All we can do at this point is follow their orders as best we can."

"But we can't just let them—"

"We don't know who 'they' are, or what 'they' want, Cass," he cut in. "The safest thing you can do for any of us is to stay put, because right now, we only know exactly where one of these bombs is, and your number one priority should be to avoid getting blown sky high. Now, stay put." He sucked in a breath, then let it go with a huffy, "Please."

Chapter Three

Cassidy watched as the man who'd once been the boy she loved walked away from her. Again. She scowled as Jake and his four-legged partner leaped from the ride and took off at a jog. Refusing to give in to nostalgia, she turned her back resolutely on the action and slumped in her seat, clamping down on her lip to keep from sinking into a full-fledged sulk.

"Two minutes."

The words echoed in her memories. It was the exact amount of time her grandmother had used to allow Cassidy to feel sorry for herself as a child. Two whole minutes to play "Oh, woe is me" before getting up and getting on with things.

But before she was even a minute into her pity party, her phone buzzed. Dread pooled in her stomach as she looked down at the notification on the screen. Another unknown number with an all-knowing message.

High noon. Glad you could never resist playing the hero.

Midnight's going to be the real banger.

High noon. Midnight.
Twelve.
A dozen.
Cassidy sucked in a sharp breath and waited for the puzzle pieces to slot into place. She read the text twice more before

pressing the button on her two-way. "Thompson, I need you and our guys to do everything you can to clear any extraneous personnel from the grounds. Tell the vendors to pack it in for the day. Cancel competition judging. Livestock and creative arts." She rubbed her forehead between her thumb and forefinger. "We need to do something about evacuating the exhibitors camping on site."

"On it," came his response.

She waited a beat then called Bud again. "And if you see Colonel Aronson from the State Police, tell him I think we have a ticking clock situation here."

Thompson's reply was terse. "Ten-four."

Setting her phone and the radio beside her on the bench seat, she tucked her chin to her chest in a vain attempt to ease the tension gathered there. It was no use. The knots forming in her shoulders only seemed to solidify the more she rolled them.

"Ma'am?"

Cassidy turned to see a fresh-faced young trooper in uniform hovering inside the cordoned area. He wore his hat pulled down to shade his eyes. Lifting a cardboard carryout container high with one hand, he took a step closer as she whirled back around.

"Captain Donovan told me to bring these to you," he said, holding a bulging plastic bag dangling from his fingers aloft.

But she lost what he said as she circled away from him. "What?"

The minute she came back around, the trooper called out, "He said you needed food and water on hand."

Cassidy stared at the younger man as she glided past. Jake sent someone to check on her in the middle of all this? The ride was moving slowly, but it was still enough to push her hair into her face. She brushed it away as she circled back to the officer.

"I, uh…" she stammered. "I don't think I can eat," she confessed. "I'm…" She made a vague circling gesture. "Yeah, probably not a good idea."

"Manny at the corn dog stand said to tell you you're better off with something in your stomach." He took a tentative step closer, then slid the container onto the nonslip metal platform between the benches with the impeccable timing of a sharpshooter. "There's some pretzel bites in here. You probably need the salt, too, ma'am."

"Trooper, you're sounding as bossy as Manny," she warned as she whirled away.

The next time she came around, he slung the bag into the same opening. "Here's the water, ma'am."

Plastic bottles wet with condensation spilled from the sack. When one attempted to roll away, Cassidy lunged, blocking the wayward bottle's escape with her foot. "Thanks. What's the situation at the north gate?"

The young trooper's jaw tightened, but she didn't have enough time to get a good read on his expression before she spun away again. "I'm not sure, ma'am. I've been assigned to stay near you."

"By your pal Donovan," she said as she came around to the front again.

"Captain Donovan. Yes, ma'am." He touched the brim of his hat like a cowboy in an old Western, then hooked a thumb over his shoulder. "I'll be within shouting distance if you need anything."

"I need information," she retorted. Leaning down to collect the water bottle, Cassidy used the cool moisture to slick her hair from her overheated face. He took a step back, preparing for retreat. "Hey, what's your name?"

"Rhodes, ma'am."

"No word of anyone hurt, Trooper Rhodes?"

"All I know is the area seemed to be clear, ma'am. The device was outside the gate."

"Damage?" she prompted.

"I can't say, but I heard the ticket booth is a goner."

She nodded as she cracked the seal on the bottle. She toasted him with her water. "Thank you."

"My pleasure, ma'am."

Cassidy took another sip of water, snatched up the food container, and turned resolutely back toward the center of the carousel. Manny wasn't wrong. She'd either feel better with something in her stomach or have something to toss up if she didn't. Either would be better than simply trying to tough this out. Besides, it sounded like they should plan for a long day and evening.

"God willing."

She opened the box and the scent of fresh bread wafted up from the container, setting her salivary glands into overdrive. Her stomach gave an ominous gurgle, but she soldiered on. The pretzel bite was still warm and pillowy. The tang of salt on her tongue made her hum in appreciation.

"Good call, Manny," she mumbled as she chewed a second nugget.

On the next rotation, she spotted Thompson speaking to the food vendor himself, both men staring worriedly at the carousel, their legs spread wide and arms crossed over their chests.

She picked up her radio. "I can see you, you know," she said through a mouthful of dough. "Get Manny out of here."

Thompson raised his radio to his mouth the next time she spun into view. "Working on it, boss."

"Tell him I'm glaring at him."

The last thing she saw as she coasted to the back of the ride was the older men raising their hands in farewell. By the time she emerged, Thompson was walking Manny and two of the other midway regulars in the direction of the south gate.

"Cass, you read me?"

The sound of Jake's new-but-all-too-familiar voice coming from her radio was disorienting. She dropped the packet of mustard she was squeezing into a pool at the corner of the container and scowled at the handset.

She narrowed her eyes, then took her time licking a smudge of mustard from her thumb before answering.

"Walker here."

"Max and I are on our way back."

She scowled and pressed the talk button hard. "Don't mind me. You go do your thing."

"This is my thing."

"Don't you have things to go sniff with your dog?"

Jake didn't respond and Cassidy immediately regretted her flippancy. She wasn't usually one to lose her cool in the midst of an emergency, but she couldn't play it cool with Jake Donovan. Hadn't been able to pull it off when she was seventeen, and apparently she hadn't developed the skill at age thirty-two.

The thud of boots hitting the metal deck followed by the scratch of toenails alerted her to their arrival. "I'm fine, Jake," she grumbled grouchily without turning around.

"I need to talk to you about the message," he said, matching her stubborn tone.

"No, I need to talk to this Aronson guy about the message."

"He sent me," he insisted.

"You must be expendable."

He appeared at the end of the bench, and she sighed heavily as she set the to-go box aside, holding a pretzel pinched between her fingers.

"I am, but Max isn't," he said in a surly tenor. "They've invested a good deal of time and money in training him."

Cassidy lowered her head, figuring it was easier to look at the dog than the man. But Max's amber gaze locked on the nugget and his jaw dropped, allowing his pink tongue to roll out like a cartoon carpet. She couldn't help but smile at the hopeful gleam in those sober eyes.

She stretched her hand out to offer the dog the tidbit, but Jake's clipped command stopped her.

"No."

She and Max tipped their heads up at the same time. Cassidy honestly wasn't sure if the word was meant for her or the dog or both. "No?"

He gave his head a quick shake. "Max doesn't eat people food. Some boiled chicken once in a while, but mostly no. It's not good for him."

The pleading look in the German shepherd's eyes said he was more than willing to experiment, but she quickly palmed the treat. "Sorry."

In one swift but not too subtle move, she tossed the pretzel over her shoulder. But rather than sailing forth onto the asphalt, it landed with a soft plunk on the metal platform. Max's yearning eyes followed the morsel's trajectory, but he made no move to go after it.

"Sorry." She spoke directly to the dog. "You are well trained."

Jake stroked the fur between the dog's enormous ears. "He's a good trooper." He dropped beside her on the bench and nodded to her phone. "What did the message say?"

"Your boss scared of merry-go-rounds or something?" she challenged.

"I think he has his hands full with the governor."

Her brows shot up. "The governor is still here?"

"Refuses to leave. Both Aronson and Hastings are coming unglued."

She sat up straighter. "He needs to listen to them. We need to get everyone who isn't security or law enforcement as far away from here as possible."

"What did the text say?"

Inhaling deeply, she held the phone between them as she read aloud. "'High noon. Glad you could never resist playing the hero. Midnight's going to be the real banger.'"

Jake stared back at her. "High noon. Midnight? What do you think they meant with the hero part?"

"I don't know." She shrugged, and padded straps tugged on her shoulders as if she needed a reminder of the bomb she wore on her back. "The backpack, I'm guessing. They had to know there was no way anyone would let a little kid walk around saddled with a bomb." She tapped on the phone screen. "But I got another message before you took off." She tapped into another thread and showed him the previous communication.

I've given you a dozen reasons. Cooperate.

"A dozen? So, we are thinking maybe twelve bombs?"

She held a palm up. "Who knows? It's possible, but the timing feels off."

Jake frowned then unzipped a pocket on Max's tactical vest. "I want to show you something." He reached inside the pocket and pulled out a plastic evidence bag.

She frowned as she eyed the red-and-white laminated We'll Be Back Soon sign with its movable clock hands pointing to straight-up twelve o'clock. "Where did you—"

"We pulled it out of the debris around the ticket booth. It was still thumbtacked to a chunk of particle board."

She was about to press him for more information, but every question she had was answered when he turned the card over to show her where someone had written "Time's up" in thick black marker on the back.

"Is this the twelve?" she asked.

He shrugged. "Possibly."

The only sound she heard as the two of them stared at the sign was the wind rushing past her ears. Or was it her pulse pounding?

"I think there are twelve bombs," she said, admitting her worst fear at last. "The timing on this might be to throw us off."

"I do, too," he agreed.

"Do you think they plan to detonate one every hour?" she mused.

His lips thinned into a tight line. "Possibly," he repeated.

Jake read the message again, then tipped his head back as if absorbing the information. "But if there are twelve and they started at noon, that only gets us up to eleven o'clock tonight."

"But midnight is going to be a real banger," she said, scooting forward and twisting to peer over her shoulder at the backpack. "This one wasn't hidden. It was handed over." She paused for a second. "To a child."

He spoke the part she couldn't bear to think about too hard aloud. "Because they knew you'd play the hero." He reached for one of the straps. "We need to get this off you."

"But they're watching," she reminded him, trying to pull away.

"But what if—" Cassidy got one arm and half the sentence out before a bang and the screech of tearing metal filled the air.

Cassidy's knee hit the deck of the carousel hard. Her breaths came in short, sharp pants as the sounds of falling debris filtered through the residual ringing in her ears.

Shattered glass. The dull clank of metal hitting the ground. Shouts. A cry of agony.

She turned her head and spotted Trooper Rhodes sprawled on the tarmac. Another man held his shoulders down as the young officer writhed in pain.

Her phone vibrated, dancing across the corrugated metal deck. She was still processing the fact that Jake had hurled his own body on top of hers, so she was slow to react. He reached for the device and held it up to her face to unlock the screen.

She vowed to herself she wouldn't point out the way he sandwiched a bomb between their bodies. He'd acted on instinct, she knew, but still she appreciated his intentions.

"Cass."

"Huh?" she managed to grunt as she uncurled her body.

"Cass, look."

The command in his tone sliced through the layer of fuzziness in her head. All of her fragmented thoughts coalesced once again as she snapped back into the here and now.

Blinking rapidly, she took it all in.

More shouts from the midway. A medic pushing people aside to get to Rhodes. Manny's corn dog stand a mess of twisted metal and broken glass. Someone shouting something about propane tanks. Boots scraping, scrambling, thumping as people ran into and away from danger.

"Cassidy," Jake said her name a third time, but this time it came out infinitely gentler.

She looked down at the screen. There, under the first two instructions the bomber had sent, they'd added a third.

Do not stop the ride.

Do not get off the ride.

Do not remove your gear, Lieutenant.

"Lieutenant again. Is it possible they know you," he said, his voice shaky with urgency.

She blinked at him, incredulous. Did he think she hadn't already gone there? Was it possible he believed she wasn't nearly as panicked as he thought she should be? Had she brought this mayhem in with her? She wagged her head in a desperate attempt to shake off some of the intrusive thoughts crowding in in on her.

"Anything's possible," she conceded at last.

"You need to think. Who could this be?"

Lieutenant. She'd spent most of her career in Security Forces.

What used to be known as Military Police. How many people had she arrested? How many careers derailed?

She clenched her jaw and swallowed hard. It wasn't her fault people couldn't keep their lives straight. She hadn't been the one who'd broken the law. All she'd done was do her job well.

"Like you, I've spent most of my career catching the bad guys." She lifted her chin in defiance. "I was good at it."

He nodded, digesting her assertion as simple fact. "Okay." He pushed himself up and brushed his hand down his vest. "While you think on that, I'm going to go check on the situation." He nodded to the mangled food concession. "Then I'm going to meet with Aronson. Can your guy get us detailed maps of the fairgrounds?"

"I've already asked Bud to supply them. Your people should have everything they need."

Jake gave a soft huff as he brushed down his pants. He peered at her, then offered his hand.

She wanted to bat it away, but then she met Max's concerned amber eyes. The dog had scrambled to his paws when his partner rose. Now he stared back at her, as earnest and eager as his partner. Jake was trying to help, and she was clinging to childhood hurts. The realization made her feel more than a little petty.

Wetting her lips, she shifted onto her hip and placed her hand in his. He hauled her to her feet and steadied her, which wasn't easy, considering the weight of the backpack and the fact they still spun in slow, sweeping circles. She stumbled into his chest, but he caught her easily, his booted feet spread wide for balance.

"Thanks." Her voice came out too breathy for her liking, but she cut herself a little slack. She was dizzier than she cared to admit to anyone, even herself.

He guided her back onto the bench and placed her phone beside her on the seat. The battery saver kicked in and the screen was black once more, but she'd never be able to erase the glaring green message bubbles from her memory.

She was the reason someone was doing this. But why? And why now? She'd been out of the service for years. Nothing made sense.

"I'm leaving Max here with you." Jake placed his hand on the dog's head.

"What? Why?" She looked from the German shepherd sitting at attention to his partner and back again.

"He's a good guard dog, and I don't think you need to be alone right now."

"But—"

He made some sort of hand gesture then pointed to her feet. "Stay." The dog turned and dropped to his haunches at the spot Jake indicated. "Listen, Max is highly trained. If he moves from this spot or give you any indication it's time to bail, I want you out of that backpack and off this ride." He jabbed a finger at her phone. "I don't care what they say."

"But shouldn't he be—"

"There's going to be plenty of time for Max to do his thing, trust me." He paused then said, "Trust him. I wasn't kidding about his training. He will sit like this until I get back, but if things start to go sideways, I want you to trust his instincts. Believe me, they're sharper than yours or mine."

Cassidy looked into the dog's solemn eyes again, then nodded. "Okay. We'll sit right here, won't we, Trooper?"

She saw Jake's shoulders lower slightly and would swear the dog leaned closer to her, but the latter might simply have been centrifugal force.

"I'll be back." He took two giant strides and leaped off the carousel.

"I've heard that line before." Cassidy watched him jog away. When she turned her attention to her canine companion, she found Max watching her with his head tilted to the side. As if he was curious about their story.

Sighing, she reached out and gave the dog an awkward pat on his head. "Same old story. He went away, and I stayed here." She leaned closer to Max and whispered into his enormous ear, "Spoiler alert. There was a time when he didn't come back."

Chapter Four

"So, what you're saying is our own head of Security is likely the target of this…" Governor Beauford paused, his hands circling as he searched for the word. "Terrorist act."

"Now, Governor—" the fair commission's media person cut in.

The governor's chief of staff piped up from the speaker on the phone the man held. "We need to choose our words carefully, Jim."

"Well, that's what we have here, isn't it?"

"What we have here is an increasingly dangerous situation, sir," Special Agent Hastings growled. "You need to leave. Now."

Before the governor could protest any more, his chief of staff and Colonel Aronson joined the chorus.

"We will keep you apprised of every development, Governor," Aronson assured him.

"You can't take this risk, Jim," his trusted advisor admonished.

"The story is already out there," the media woman reported. "Of course this had to happen today of all days."

The governor turned on her. "You think tomorrow would be better? When the gates are open and thousands of innocent people—families—are here trying to enjoy a day of wholesome fun?"

They devolved into a spirited debate over which scenario was worse, and Jake turned away. He peered through the glass doors of the arena, squinting in the direction of the midway, but he couldn't see the carousel. And the longer he was away, the more fidgety he became.

When he turned back, the chief of staff was speaking again. "If you get yourself blown up, Polly will have my hide. And you know Morrisey is practically salivating at the thought of being sworn in."

Jake bit the inside of his cheek. They didn't have time for posturing and finger-pointing. The clock was ticking. He leaned into Furst, who'd stepped up beside him in the circle. "Is there an update on Trooper Rhodes?"

The firefighter nodded. "EMS treated multiple cuts and lacerations on site. Embedded foreign objects and debris. They suspect concussion. He's suffering some hearing loss—hopefully temporary—and possibly some internal bleeding. They've got him at the trauma center now."

A sober silence had descended as he gave the recitation. When Jake looked back at the small knot of people, he made eye contact with the governor, and the man gave a grim nod.

"Fine." The governor turned to Colonel Aronson. "But I expect you to be in close contact. I want more than updates. I want details."

"Yes, sir."

Agent Hastings gestured to the concourse leading to the opposite side of the arena. "Right this way. The car is at the east gate."

With a final nod, the governor swiveled and his security detail closed in around him. Jake and the other officers watched as Beauford strode away, spouting orders and threats of minor mayhem to his closest advisor.

The moment the bigwigs left, the assembled officers heaved a sigh. "Okay, let's get going," Colonel Aronson said, clapping his hands once to command their attention. "Donovan. Tell us what you have."

"Confirmed explosive device in the pack Ms. Walker took from the little boy." He hesitated, searching for the kid's name. "Darien."

"And it's your belief she took it from him knowing the bag was suspicious?"

Jake nodded. "I witnessed the exchange."

"And what did Ms. Walker say? Why did she take the backpack?"

"She had already received the first messages, sir," Jake reminded him. "There was a credible bomb threat. There was a little boy wearing a pack a stranger gave to him under the pretext it contained a gaming console all the other kids would want."

One of the Little Rock police officers shifted from one foot to the other. "Sick jerk."

"Exactly," Jake concurred. "This is someone who doesn't care if they're using an innocent child or harming anyone who gets in their way. "

"I have people running background on Ms. Walker. You said you thought the perp may have ties to her military service?" Aronson prompted.

"The messages refer to her service rank more than once. They clearly have an agenda and, at the moment, they have the edge."

The commander leaned in. "Okay." He stared down at the detailed map of the fairgrounds spread on a folding table in front of him. "Let's figure out who's doing this so we can turn the tables on them."

JAKE AND MEMBERS of the local bomb squads from both Little Rock and North Little Rock gathered around a duplicate of Aronson's map a few minutes later.

Jake smoothed the folds in the glossy paper so it lay as flat as possible. "We have the better part of a dozen devices to find, and possibly a ticking clock."

He bit down on the cap of a black marker, pulled it open and held the cap clenched between his teeth as he circled the north gate and the area where the wreckage of the corn dog stand still smoldered. Sliding the marker back into its cap, he used both hands to tighten it.

"Best guesses?" he prompted, looking from man to man.

Without hesitation, each began marking up the map. Once they'd identified a handful of sites they all agreed were prime locations, the group split up with their respective teams and the hunt began.

Map in hand, Jake hoofed it back to the carnival midway. With the kids, media and workers gone, the place was even more deserted than when he'd first arrived. In all his years with the State Police, he'd never worked the fair in any capacity. It was strange to walk past games of chance and not be taunted into giving them a try. Disturbing to see all the rides at a standstill. Except one.

With the music turned off, he could hear every squeak and creak of the crankshafts simulating the motion of horses jumping. Others simply clawed at the air with their hooves. The hum of generators reminded him of the steady drone of cicadas in late summer.

Cassidy had tipped her head back and closed her eyes, but he didn't believe for one second she was as relaxed as she appeared. She couldn't possibly be. Still, she didn't stir when he moved the section of barrier fencing directly in his path aside. Jake hopped onto the moving ride and strode to the bench flanked by gaudy blue-green seahorses. Max turned to look but didn't move from his post at her feet.

He gave the dog a pat. "Good boy."

"Got it all in hand?" Cass didn't open her eyes.

He dropped onto the bench across from her and Max immediately switched allegiance. "I brought a map," he said, dispensing with preamble. "I wanted to go over some possibilities with you."

She shook her head. "Can't right now. I feel like hurling."

Jake pressed his lips together, swallowing hard as he tried to imagine how awful she must feel. She'd been whirling for well over an hour, and who knew how many more she'd have to go.

"I'm going to find you some paper bags or something in case you need to be sick."

She raised one hand in acknowledgment, then let it fall limply in her lap. "Manny was right. Having something in my stomach helps, but I don't think I can read much while I'm on this thing."

Jake's mind flashed to a memory. Cassidy feeling carsick as she sat in the passenger seat of his third-hand Honda, pleading with him to slow down as she painstakingly tried to type out a message on her phone. "Still get carsick?"

She opened her eyes. And then she rolled them before letting them close again. "Who me? Nah."

Jake couldn't stifle the startled chuckle that escaped him. This grown-up version of the girl he'd once known looked much the same, and somehow totally different. It was oddly comforting to know her droll sense of humor remained unchanged.

He let his smile stretch as another moment came rushing back to him. "Remember when we drove up to the Buffalo to go floating and you totally lost it outside Marshall?"

"Jake," she said.

"What? I get it, the road was curvy."

She opened her eyes again, but the good-natured humor he expected to see there was apparently wishful thinking on his part. Her expression was neutral, but her glare was sharp and forbidding. "We're not going there," she said without heat.

"I, uh—" Ducking his head, he stared at the map he'd folded back into a neat rectangle. He bit his bottom lip as he took a moment to adjust to the knowledge that Cassidy Walker was not as happy to see him again as he was to see her. "No. Right. Of course." He drew in a deep breath. "Sorry."

"A blanket apology?"

"I'm not…" He frowned as he tried to figure out what she thought he needed to be sorry for in addition to broaching the subject of their past but then shook it off. "Sure," he conceded with a decisive nod. "Sorry for everything."

She gave a soft snort when she laughed. "Your sincerity is overwhelming."

"Yeah, well, consider it a blanket, too," he shot back.

Desperate to focus on a slightly less-volatile topic, he chose to talk incendiary devices. "I've got teams checking the areas around some of the bigger rides—the swings, the spinner, the pirate ship," he said as he unfolded the map. "I've also got people sweeping the food court area and the Hall of Industry." He turned the map and stared hard at the building where local businesses could come to hawk their services trade-show style. "I was thinking the petting zoo area would be good," he ventured.

"Don't forget the stages," she interrupted. "The main pavilion next to the Hall of Industry. There's a smaller setup across from the cattle barn."

"Have you thought any more about the number twelve?"

She huffed a laugh. "Don't you mean have I thought about anything other than the number twelve?"

"Are the buildings numbered? I mean, aside from the designations on the signs, is there any kind of internal numbering system?"

She opened her eyes and studied him for a long, searching minute. She opened her mouth as if to speak, then clamped down on her bottom lip as she shook her head.

"What if I count twelve buildings in from the gate?" he suggested.

Her brow furrowed as she considered the suggestion. "Which gate?"

He shrugged. "I guess we'll start with the north since who-ever is doing this started there."

"Permanent structures only?"

"Gotta start somewhere."

Without even glancing at the map, she started to tick them off on her fingers. "Box Office. Main Stage. Diner. Industry. Arts. Cattle 1. Cattle 2. Barton. Cattle 3. Cattle 4. Bud's Burg-ers. The Arkansas Building…" She stopped.

He pulled the marker from his back pocket and circled the Arkansas Building on the map. "Okay. And if we go south to north?"

"Equestrian Center. Rabbits. Goats and Sheep. Poultry. Horses. Arkansas. Horse 2. Swine Barn. Bud's. Cattle 4. Cat-tle 3. Barton Coliseum," she recited.

"We've swept Barton," he reminded her.

"Then Cattle 2, I guess." She shook her head as if they'd al-ready set out on a hopeless quest. "There are a lot of other barns and outbuildings in there."

"But these are the ones most people would know, right?"

"Right."

"Then we'll start with them." He rose and took up Max's lead. "I have one of your radios on me. If you hear anything else, you—"

He was cut off midsentence by the police radio clipped to his vest. "Got a hot potato," one of the other members of the combined tactical team reported.

Colonel Aronson returned the call. "Team and location?"

Jake and Cassidy listened attentively as the information was exchanged. "Brusk and Hollins, LRPD. We have a visual on an IED planted beneath the pirate ship, sir."

Aronson's response was clipped but congratulatory. "Good work. Backup and tech support on their way."

Cassidy looked up to find Jake staring at her. "Number

three," he said with a slow nod. "Maybe we'll get lucky and sniff them all out."

She gave nervous harrumph of a laugh. "Wouldn't that be great?"

"We strive for greatness," he said as he gave Max a pat. "What do you say, partner? Wanna go hunting?"

Max responded with a short, sharp bark and they moved to the edge of the ride. Jake turned back before he leaped and was surprised to find she'd followed them. He had to go. Time was passing. Plus, he wasn't exactly sure what she wanted from him. Comfort? Reassurance? In the end, he settled for saying simply, "Hang in there, Cass. We're going to figure this out."

With that, he hopped down. The moment his boots hit the ground, she called after him. "Keep me updated on what they found!"

Jake shielded his eyes with his hand, looking in the direction of the ride designed to look like a pirate ship swung like a pendulum. "I'll let you know if I hear anything, but you can figure no boom is good news."

When she swung by him again, he caught her pointed scowl. Snapping off a smart salute, he hollered, "If they can't disarm it, they may opt for a controlled detonation. If they do, I'll be sure to let you know."

"Yes, please," she said as she circled past. He's almost cleared the temporary fencing before she shouted an anxious-sounding, "Hey, Jake?"

He reeled around, pulling the lead taut in an attempt to curb Max's impatience. "Yeah?"

"Look out for my friend Max, will you?"

He smiled and gave the dog a few inches more on the lead. "You obviously don't know him well. He's the one who looks out for me."

Without allowing himself one more glance back at her, he broke into a trot, his partner easily keeping pace at his side. A small smile tugged at the corner of his mouth as he headed up the hill to the string of barns designated for cattle. Judging had been underway for days, according to Bud Thompson. The moment he started up the hill, Jake's nose was assaulted by proof.

He slowed to a walk, giving himself time to adjust to the combined scents of cow, hay and manure. By the time he and Max stood at the opening to Cattle Barn 3, he was almost acclimated to it.

Almost.

Jake's stomach roiled, but the dog was drinking it all in, his snout held high, damp nostrils flaring as his superior olfactory receptors took in every layer of the pungent odor. He could almost see Max's mind working as the dog sniffed and snuffled, pawing the straw-strewn concrete as he parsed the pungent cocktail.

"Ready?" The question was completely inane. His partner was fairly quivering with excitement. He was a stink glutton at the world's smelliest buffet. A massive brown-and-white heifer chewed methodically as she eyeballed them from the nearest stall. At last, he unclipped Max's lead. "Okay, have at it, but try not to get trampled."

He hung back, watching as his partner moved from one stall to the next, unperturbed by the massive occupants, and undeterred when an Angus objected to his nosiness. Jake followed as Max methodically made his way down the long, narrow section. When they reached the opening at the end, the dog circled back to work his way along the other side of the building.

Max truly was the more useful of the two of them.

When they ended up back where they'd started, Jake clipped the lead to his partner's harness again and stepped out into the magically fresh air of the breezeway. Eying the length of the aisle they'd inspected, Jake herded the dog toward the concrete steps. "Sorry, boy. I need a little outside time."

They made their way down the path to the next cattle barn,

where once again, Jake let Max take the lead. The dog hadn't made it two stalls in before he let out a sharp bark and bolted for a stall currently occupied by a Texas longhorn.

"You have got to be kidding me." Jake moved closer, his eyes narrowing.

The enormous bovine chewed contentedly on a mouthful of Bermuda hay, despite the sign indicating the next feeding time for cattle would not take place until six in the evening. The animal's fabled horns stretched at least two feet in each direction. Not as big as some he'd seen on TV, but still impressive. Perhaps she wasn't fully grown, he speculated as he stepped cautiously around the opening of the stall.

The heifer was tethered and didn't seem to be the least bit bothered by the dog dancing around the bales of straw piled inside the wall. Jake eyed the cow's rear hooves and massive hindquarters. She was obviously accustomed to people moving in and out of the stall, but they were not her people, and he could write everything he knew about handling cattle on his thumbnail.

His partner sat down next to a stack of baled straw and gave three short barks.

"Gotcha." He whistled for Max and fell back a few steps before pressing the button. "I have a K-9 positive ID. Cattle Barn 4." He tipped his head and verified the stall number. "Stall 2. Currently in use by a Texas longhorn by the name of…Augusta. Owned by Samuel Perkins, 4-H Hempstead County."

There was a moment of crackling static, then someone guffawed. "No bull?"

Jake rolled his eyes as he headed for the barn's opening. He recognized the voice of one of the leads from the State Police Tactical Unit. He also knew the boss would recognize the cocky tone as well. "Sounds like I have a volunteer. Come on down, Winter."

"No one here by that name."

"Got a sweet little heifer waiting for you at Cattle Barn 4," Jake said. "See you in a minute."

"Now, Cap—" The man groaned.

"Winter, get over there," Colonel Aronson cut in. "Maybe next time you won't be so quick to go for the cheap chuckle."

Max danced restlessly beside him. "Yes, yes, I know." Jake extracted a piece of a treat from his own vest pocket. The dog instantly dropped to his haunches, still as an overstimulated canine could be. "You are the best, boy. The very best."

Max chomped twice on the treat, then gulped it down, turning back to Jake the moment the snack was a memory.

"Hang tight, buddy." He knelt to look his partner straight in the eye as he spoke in a soothing tone. "You did great. Once Sergeant Smartypants gets here to do some cleanup, we'll go check out the Arkansas Building. We'll see if you can find some more."

"I swear, you and that pooch of yours should exchange rings and call it official," Sergeant Mark Winter said as he and two men from his team pulled up in a golf cart.

"He's too good for me," Jake said, rising to meet his old friend and his cohorts. "Nice ride."

"Gets us around." Winter's grin stretched his cheeks, carving deep parentheses between his mouth and the straps of his tactical helmet. They shook hands, then Winter extended his gloved knuckles to Max. The dog bumped them with his muzzle, then turned his attention back to the stall where the cow was still casually chomping away.

"Whoa. Big animal." Winter craned his neck to get a better look at Augusta.

"We gotta get her out of there, Sarge." One of the other men, a freckle-faced young man who didn't yet look capable of sprouting a full beard, brushed past them into the barn. "If she gets spooked while we're in there, it's bad news. Not to mention, she's worth a lot of money," he added, wrinkling his nose as he turned back to them.

Jake and Winter exchanged a look, eyebrows raised. Winter's grin returned. "Sounds like you know something about cows, Miller."

"Grew up on a farm outside Valley Springs." The younger man shrugged.

"Good. You're in charge of taking Miss...uh—"

"Augusta," Jake interjected.

"—to safer quarters while we work." He grimaced as he checked out the stalls around the opening of the building and saw they were all in use. "As a matter of fact, we may need to move a few of them, to be safe."

"Hang on," Jake said. He pulled the security department's radio from his vest pocket and stepped back as he made the call. "Cass, you read me?"

Chapter Five

Cassidy jumped when she heard his voice calling her name. She'd been focusing on one of the gilt-edged mirrors on the hub at the center of the ride. She could no longer keep her eyes shut, and turning around to watch the world whizzing past was completely out of the question. She honestly didn't know how much longer she could handle staying on, no matter what her instructions said.

Jake's call was exactly the distraction she needed. "Copy. What have you got?"

"Cattle Barn 4 is on the hot list. We need to move some of the residents as a precaution." There was a pause, as if he was listening to someone else, then he was back again. "About six to eight head of cattle. Any idea where we can park them?"

She nodded as she digested what he was telling her. They'd found another bomb. The fifth, counting the one on her back. Not bad for a couple hours' work.

"I, uh…" She squinted her eyes shut, gave her head a decisive shake, willing logic to break through the fog of fear and nausea. "There's an auxiliary building," she blurted.

Then she took a deep breath and forced herself to speak in complete and coherent sentences. "On the other side of the Coliseum," she said, her voice growing stronger as the plan took shape. "Thompson, you read?"

"Already heading in that direction," the older man responded. "I'll scoop up Witchell on the way."

"Jake, Bud and Ed Witchell will help get the cattle moved. Ed oversees security around the livestock. He should be able to round up a hand or two to help."

There was a pause before Jake answered. "Ten-four. I have a team here to work on the device. Max and I are heading for the Arkansas Building."

Bile rose in her throat as she let the information sink in. Jake and Max had found the bomb. There were explosives planted all around her fairgrounds and they hadn't the faintest idea what the perpetrator's game plan was. She glanced at her watch and saw it was nearly one o'clock.

Biting down on her lip, she did her best to quell the panic clawing up her throat as she spoke into the radio. "It's nearly one," she said, her voice quavering. "You want to hold off until the top of the hour passes?"

Her voice rose on the last part of the suggestion, turning it into a question. Cassidy hated sounding so unsure but, at the moment, there was no controlling it. She was sitting on a spinning ride with a bomb strapped to her back. She figured she had every right to feel scared and uncertain.

"Good call," Jake said. "I'll relay."

Cassidy turned her head, searching out another spot at the center of the ride she could latch on to while Jake conferred with the other members of law enforcement. She wanted to be looped in. When Jake came back on, she'd insist on having access to their radio communications. There was no way she was sitting here being spoon-fed bits of buffed and polished information like she was some kind of victim to be protected.

But she wasn't. She was stuck on this stupid ride all by herself. Synced up with no one.

She closed her eyes and exhaled. "Two minutes."

In those brief minutes, she allowed herself to feel the weight of being both the victim and the probable target in this mess. She gave herself over to the thrumming headache at the base of her skull and acknowledged the churning in her gut. The urge to plug her ears with her fingers was nearly unbearable. She wasn't sure what it would do for her—block out the wind, keep every intrusive thought she was having trapped inside, or maybe stop things up so she imploded before she exploded? Curling her fingers into fists, she clamped her jaw tight and began humming. At first, it was tuneless, something to drown out the panic. But within a minute, it morphed into a pop song. One she and Jake used to mockingly belt out as it played at full volume in his car. A song she secretly loved.

"Ma'am?"

She opened her eyes to see a slim man wearing cargo pants and a navy T-shirt proclaiming him to be a LRFD Trainee standing near the carousel. He wore the curved brim of his LRFD cap pulled over his eyes, but the lines fanning from them told her he was squinting against the bright sunlight.

"Yes?"

"Can I get you anything? Water? Food?"

He sounded hopeful. Eager to help. It reminded her of Trooper Rhodes, and her stomach curdled. "No. Thank you," she added with weak smile. "I'm okay."

"If you need anything, let me know. I'll be around," he assured her.

"I appreciate you." He turned to go, and she had a flash of Trooper Rhodes doing the exact same thing. "Hey," she called to him. "What's your name?"

When she came around again, she caught the tail end of a self-effacing shrug. "Everyone calls me T.B."

She nodded and raised a hand as she spun toward the back again. "Thanks, T.B."

Closing her eyes again, she ignored the ever-present rush of wind in her ears and concentrated on taking air in. After three cycles of box breathing, her heartbeat finally slowed, only to have it kick up when the platform shook beneath her.

"Cass?"

Her eye sprang open and the first thing she saw was the time displayed on her phone: 12:59. Then she focused on the pair of boots in her peripheral vision and the gold-brown paws beside them.

"I thought you were supposed to be falling back until after the top of the hour." She practically spat the words at him, her heart hammering with fear and anticipation.

"We are." Jake sat down beside her.

"If you haven't noticed, one of the bombs is on this ride," she reminded him tightly.

"I have a feeling that one is the midnight special. This is probably the safest place on the grounds."

Cassidy recognized the stubborn streak in his tone, and she couldn't say she was sad to hear it. The noble thing to do would be to send Jake and his gorgeous dog as far away from her as they could possibly get. But she wasn't feeling noble. Or brave. Plus, she agreed. The bomb she carried was probably meant to be the finale in this pyrotechnics display.

After clearing the lump of emotion from her throat, she asked, "Where are we at with everything?"

"We disarmed the device at the pirate ship. They'll start working on the cattle barn location once the animals are moved. Max and I are waiting to check the—"

An explosion at the south end of the grounds shattered the relative calm.

Cassidy stared at the smoke rising into the air, mentally calculating proximity and the possibilities of people working nearby.

"Arkansas Building." She turned, needing to see him. What if she'd hallucinated his return? What if he and Max—

"What?" Jake tore his attention from the teams running past them toward the blast site.

She bobbed her head in the direction of the explosion but

couldn't take her eyes off him. Wetting parched lips, she spoke again. "I'm afraid that may have been the Arkansas Build—"

His radio squawked to life. It seemed like every user was trying to talk at once. Finally, Colonel Aronson's baritone broke through the noise. "Arkansas Building. Let Fire through first."

Jake started to rise, and for the first time, wobbled a bit. He hit the bench seat beside her hard, his eyes wide with realization.

He and Jake would have been in there if she hadn't reminded them of the possibility of a countdown. Cassidy's stomach did a full somersault as they stared at one another, comprehension dawning.

"Twelve o'clock and now one."

"Another bomb located."

He continued to stare at her, but his eyes were unfocused. Pensive. As if he were searching his memory for a clue he wasn't quite sure was there. Eager to help him along, she dove into her theories.

"Okay, so not in a numerical pattern." He tipped his head quizzically, and she shrugged. "North gate, midway, livestock barns, now a building on the south end." She pointed in each direction.

"We got some of it right, counting buildings," he countered.

Cassidy nodded but wrinkled her nose. "Might have been luck. Or process of elimination."

"Let's settle for an educated guess." Jake turned back toward the action, his expression tense with impatience.

"Go," she said, making a shooing motion.

She'd captured his full attention again. "What? No."

"You're clearly dying to be in the thick of it, and there's no point in you staying here."

He flexed his jaw as he mulled. "There's no point in me going there," he concluded flatly. "Max and I do detection and identification."

She pursed her lips as she took in his explanation. "Then you need more places to look."

He let out a sigh as he gave Max's head a reassuring pat. "I guess so."

"Is someone checking the Arts and Crafts Building?" Cassidy plowed ahead without waiting for a response. "It's open space in there, aside from the display cases, but there is an office and a kitchen."

Jake nodded as he digested the information. "Good to know."

"The Hall of Industry is a blank slate aside from the bathrooms and the concession area." When he didn't move or give any indication he'd heard her, she jabbed him with her elbow. "Wanna write this down?"

He turned to look directly at her, his face a mask of concern. "What happens if the bombs we're dismantling were scheduled for two or three o'clock?"

She assumed he was merely musing aloud, but the impulse to answer his possibility with one of her own was strong. Her lips parted, but the thought died on her tongue as she absorbed the unspoken questions layered beneath the one he'd asked. It was entirely possible they were working their way to an expedited end to their situation, but it might not be the best overall outcome. Particularly not for her.

"You think they'd retaliate if one doesn't explode?" But they both already knew the answer.

"Look what they did when we tried to get you out of the backpack."

She turned in the direction of the mangled corn dog stand, sighing as the ride carried them past, then holding her breath until she caught sight of the twisted food trailer again.

"They could set them all off." Cassidy spoke through fear-numb lips.

He closed his eyes and angled his head back. Apparently, this posture disturbed his partner, because Max shifted closer to rest his large muzzle on Jake's knee. She watched as Jake's fingers skimmed over his partner's sleek head, wondering if he was soothing the dog, or if petting the dog comforted him. Probably both, she concluded.

"The other option is to do nothing and see how things play out."

"Not an option. This fair is set to open tomorrow. For the first time in years, we have good weather. We could have record attendance. We can't risk anyone getting hurt."

The alarm she'd been tamping down since this whole fiasco started bubbled up inside her. She turned and looked him straight in the eye. "I can't be the reason whoever this is ruins everything."

Her phone buzzed with an incoming text. She picked it up from the bench and flipped it over. Another unknown number displayed in her notifications. When she opened the app, another taunt punched her right in the gut.

Always by the book. I'm making the rules now, Walker.

Cassidy wanted to moisten her wind-chapped lips, but all she could do was mash them together. A hot rush of tears threatened, and the last thing she wanted was to break down in front of Jake Donovan. She hadn't at eighteen, and she wasn't about to give him the satisfaction now. Throat dry and tight, she turned the screen so he could see it.

Their gazes met and locked.

Jake swallowed hard, then straightened his shoulders. "Right. Well, we're going to beat them at their own game."

"I don't know how much longer I can do this," she said, her voice barely more than a scratchy whisper.

Jake eyed her appraisingly. After a long moment, he gave a single nod. "Oh, I'm sure you can."

Her mouth opened but no words came out. She could not

imagine how he'd come to have such faith in her. He didn't know her at all anymore. And after this was over—

"I need to get you a charging block," he said. He retracted the phone from her grip and hit the button to turn off the display. "Save your battery as much as you can."

"I keep a couple of magnetic chargers in my office. Didn't think I'd need it today, but during the fair…" She let the words trail off with a grimace when he handed her mobile back. "Funny, I didn't plan to be held hostage by a mad bomber today."

The corner of his mouth twisted into a small smile as he pulled the police radio from his vest. "Ask one of your guys to grab them."

Cassidy relayed the request to Thompson, who was the only member of her team with a key to her office.

Jake turned to survey the carnival midway as it whizzed past them. "Anyone have a status on the detonation site?" he asked into his radio.

"Contained," Aronson replied. "No injuries. Property damage. This one packed more of a punch than the others."

He reclipped the radio. "Okay, so we have identified six of what we think may be a dozen devices." He leaned back, his expression calm but focused solely on her. "Let's start at the beginning. What do we know?"

She quirked an eyebrow at his leading tone, but she understood exactly what he was doing. By breaking their situation down into increments, they might be able to parse more clues. She picked up her phone and opened her notes app. "I'm going to copy the messages in sequence. Maybe seeing them all together will give us a better sense of how things have unfolded."

Jake nodded approvingly. "Great idea." He pulled the map of the fairgrounds from his vest pocket. "Go low, Max."

Despite the easygoing manner with which he delivered the command, the dog obeyed, immediately stretching out on his stomach at their feet.

"Such a good dog." She didn't look up as she copied and pasted each of the texts she'd received into a single document.

"I remember Muffin."

Cassidy stilled, thrown off-kilter by his offhand reference to her childhood dog. Muffin had been her black Labrador retriever with a love of cheese and disdain for all forms of exercise, but she'd been sweet and loving, and would allow the mere mortals who served her to scratch behind her ears as much as they wanted.

Jake's father had been allergic, so his family had never kept pets, thus he'd doted on her dog. Cassidy had little doubt in her mind he'd probably been more upset by the prospect of breaking it off with Muffin than with her. Still, there was no reason to rehash ancient history.

Without looking up from her task, she said, "She was a sweet girl."

"Remember how she'd go around lying on everyone's feet in the winter?"

She heard a smile caught up in the memory but couldn't chance a glance to see it. Jake had loved her dog and remembered her fondly. The tug she felt in her belly was nothing more than motion sickness.

"She was a funny one."

A full minute passed before he spoke again. "If we're out in the car when they test the emergency sirens on Wednesdays, Max howls along."

This tidbit was too much. She tore her attention from her screen but refused to look at Jake. Instead, she gazed down at Max, whose ears twitched as if catching every syllable they uttered.

"Are you in touch with your inner wolf, Max?" she crooned.

The dog gave her a sheepish side-eye, and she chucked. "I don't blame you. I like to howl along with them, too."

Jake laughed. "I bet you do."

His chuckles proved too captivating to resist. She met his bright blue eyes and her heart began to thrum against her breastbone. Needing to regain some traction, she raised both eyebrows. "Because I'm a dog?"

She regretted the flippant comment as soon as she spoke it. His laughter died out, the dregs of it carried away on the breeze. The light in his eyes dimmed and a deep crease bisected his eyebrows. "What? No."

His voice was tinged with such utter disbelief, she felt small and petty. Like she'd been fishing for compliments. She shook her head dismissively and went back to her task, unable to look directly at him. "Never mind. Sorry. Bad joke."

But it hadn't been a joke. She wanted to know if he thought she was pretty. She wanted to know how he'd walked away from her so easily when they were kids. The yearning to ask him for reasons and explanations was nearly as strong as it had been all those years ago. But, thankfully, so was her pride.

"Where are you checking next?"

"I, uh…" His voice broke, and he stopped to clear his throat. When he spoke again, his voice was deep and cool, totally in control. "I was thinking of checking the other livestock buildings and show ring."

When he didn't elaborate, she knew he was waiting for her input on his plan. Forcing herself to look up, she did her best to keep her tone casual. "Yeah?"

Jake nodded. "I think…" He stopped and turned to stare unseeingly at the maze of trailers and cables cluttering the rear of the carnival setup. "If they wanted to hurt people, they could have done it by now. We know, or we are pretty sure, they're watching, right?"

She nodded, liking his line of reasoning.

"It might be they can only see this area, but who's to say they haven't been watching all the locations. The two detonations went off in unoccupied spaces."

Her lips thinned into a grim line as a vision of Trooper Rhodes laid out on the asphalt appeared in her mind's eye. "Except for the corn dog stand."

"Which I think was an impulse," he countered. "A warning shot to keep us in line."

She bobbed her head slowly as she took in his theory. "But you think they wouldn't have any trouble harming animals," she concluded flatly.

Jake pulled a face, then shrugged. "I don't know. Maybe not." He exhaled loudly, his shoulders slumping. "I mean I'd hate to think so, but the reality is most of the cattle will be sold for stud or steak."

She winced at the colloquialism but could not find fault with his reasoning. The animals shown at the fair were not pets. Oh, sure, some of the younger kids and teens showing may have formed attachments with the specimens they raised, but almost all farm kids were well acquainted with the harsh outcomes most livestock would face.

Taking a deep breath, she inclined her head in acquiescence. "Okay. Sounds like a plan." She pasted the last of the messages into her collection, then extended the device to him. "Here, text this to yourself and anyone else you think might be good at reading between the lines."

Jake took the phone and began typing as he talked. "I'll send it to myself and forward it to Aronson. He can decide who needs to see it. I don't want to clutter your inbox any more than we have to."

She heard the faint ping of a notification, but he kept tapping on the screen rather than relinquishing her phone. Cocking her head, she raised a challenging brow. "Forget your own number?"

"I'm putting all my contact information in, so you know when it's me calling." He frowned at the screen then, apparently satisfied, saved the information. "I know it's not the cool thing to do, but if you need me or I need you, let's call. It's faster than typing."

She took her phone back and saw he'd saved his information as a "favorite" in her address book. "Fairly sure of yourself," she said as he and his partner got to their feet.

"What do you mean?"

"You made yourself a favorite," she explained.

His smile flashed as quick and lethal as a bolt of lightning. "Well, a guy can hope."

She gaped at his back as he and Max moved to the edge of the platform, preparing to jump. Jake's boots slapped the ground, but Max's landing was as graceful as a dancer's. "Hope for what?"

"Better days," Jake answered without looking back.

She stared after him for a moment, then quickly gathered her scattered senses. "Hey!" When Jake turned, she pointed to the east. "Start with the poultry and work your way west. Let me know where you're at."

He fired off a smirk and a salute, then turned on his heel with a brusque, "Ma'am, yes, ma'am!"

Cassidy sank back on the bench, trying to ignore the hollow feeling in her chest as she watched him go.

Chapter Six

He stole one last peek at Cass then spoke into his radio. Every time he had to walk away, his footsteps felt heavier. He hated leaving her alone there with that bag strapped to her back. But he had a job to do, and if he did it well, maybe he could get her out of this mess sooner rather than later. "I'm heading to the Poultry Barn. Anyone have a chance to check Cattle 1 and 2 yet?"

Aronson replied after a moment's pause. "I sent Stephens and his team in. Winter's crew is heading in to disarm building four."

"Thank you, sir. Swinging by to see if the fire guys found anything interesting at the Arkansas Building on the way, then Max and I will work our way west through the other livestock buildings."

"Ten-four. Solid plan. When the team in Industry finishes up, I'll send them through the horse barns," Aronson confirmed.

Jake's steps slowed as he hiked up the incline away from the midway. The Arkansas Building was built out of bricks but sported a gently curved roofline reminiscent of an old barn. Signs staked into the patch of grass announced a number of pageants and talent contests scheduled for the coming week. A concrete ramp sloped gently down to a pair of glass doors, which stood propped open wide.

The glass in one door was shattered like a spider's web but appeared to be holding for the moment. He could see LRFD personnel moving around inside the dim space, but something about the doors niggled at him. He was eying the shattered one when a firefighter in turnout gear approached with a wide roll of masking tape in hand. He affixed one end of the tape to the corner of the door and pulled the tape diagonally across the broken glass.

"How bad is it?" Jake peered past the man's shoulder. All he could make out was a jumble of chairs tossed around and what appeared to be the smoldering remains of a stage blown to pieces.

The firefighter shrugged. "Could have been worse. Someone could have been in there."

A shiver ran down Jake's spine. He would have been the someone if Cass hadn't reminded him of their theory about hourly detonations. Unsettled by the thought, he checked the time on his watch again. A quarter past one already. The day was slipping away.

Backing up, he nodded to the firefighter. "We're heading to check out one of the barns. Take care in there."

The other man saluted him then smiled at Max before he set about stretching another length of tape starting at the opposite corner. "You, too."

Jake set off again, veering from the paved path to cut across another stretch of gras and up a steep hill. He passed the Rabbit Barn without glancing in. He and Max would barely have time to get through the chickens and turkeys before they needed to fall back again before the clock struck two.

Imagining the top of the hour made his mind leap to Cass. He hadn't strayed far from thoughts of her since the second he'd clapped eyes on her. Cassidy Walker, all grown up and even prettier than she'd been in high school.

And even back then, she was the prettiest girl he'd ever seen.

Cass always had an easy, natural way about her. Sure, she

wore makeup and all the trendy clothes the other girls wore, but on her everything seemed kind of…effortless.

Her hair was the same buttered-toast color he remembered. Freckles still speckled her nose. Not a lot of them, but enough to be an integral part of her. He'd loved when she wrinkled her nose at something he said. The tantalizing flecks of brown would compress then expand, forming new constellations for him to study every time he looked at her. He'd loved her sass and her smile, and the saucy little wink she'd give him every time they passed in the hall at school. He could see her as she was then, all carefree confidence and playful swagger, her backpack dangling off one shoulder as she made her way to her next class.

Her backpack.

They'd been required to carry mesh bags in those days. The heavy-duty nylon canvas, like the one she bore today, would have been banned for exactly the reason she wore it today.

Max pulled up at the entrance to the barn, his ears pricked and his head upturned, awaiting Jake's command to run into danger. And the dog would do it. Not only willingly, but happily, because this was what they trained for. Max had exactly two happy places—at home and at work. And they were here to work, not obsess over the girl—woman—he thought he'd never see again.

Looking into Max's expectant eyes, Jake took a moment to center himself. The building was empty except for the birds. For any other dog, they might prove to be a distraction, but Jake knew his partner was too well trained to let his attention stray from the task at hand. The previous year, they'd investigated a bomb threat an animal rights group had called in at one of the poultry processing plants in the northwest part of the state, and Max had performed admirably.

Leaning down, he thumbed the breakaway clip on the lead. "All business, my friend. Don't forget all your expensive schooling." He unclipped the leash, but Max didn't make a break for it.

He stood still, aside from the telltale quiver of muscles bunching beneath his thick fur. "Go," Jake ordered in an urgent tone, and he was off.

Jake walked slowly into the dim light of the barn, blinking until his eyes adjusted. To his left, Max worked his way methodically along the west wall of the building. Birds in cages stacked three and four high squeaked and squawked. Each cage was labeled with a white card in a laminated pouch zip-tied to its bars. Jake moved to the bank of cages straight ahead of them, his lips quirking into an involuntary smile as a cadre of chickens clucked and cooed their greetings.

"Hello there, uh…" He peered at the card in the plastic sleeve. It proclaimed them commercial laying hens. "Ladies." He gave them a nod as he moved down the row. "Thanks for breakfast."

Max was already circling back to make a pass at the first aisle of stacked cages. The clucking and chirruping seemed to grow louder as the birds became inured to their presence. The noise set his teeth on edge.

Acting on impulse, he pulled out the radio Bud Thompson had given him. "The chicken barn is a little creepy," he said without preamble.

Cass answered with a chuckle. "Bud's scared of it, too."

Thompson piped up almost immediately. "I'm not scared of it, but I don't like it."

"It's the eyes." Jake followed Max into the next aisle. "Beady eyes."

"Like they're watching your every move and reporting on it," Thompson agreed.

"I'm beginning to wonder who the real chickens are," Cass teased.

He could hear the smile in her voice and picture it perfectly in his mind's eye. It was embarrassing how far that went toward making him feel better.

"We're heading to the kids' area," Thompson informed him.

He'd attached himself to a couple of LRPD investigators he said he knew from his days on the force, and Jake was glad. While the assembled teams certainly needed his expertise when it came to knowing the lay of the land, they were all functioning in their preordained units. Colonel Aronson believed people worked better with fewer outside influences in the mix, and Jake agreed.

He and Max did their best work on their own. They'd melt into the larger tactical team as needed, but for the most part, they preferred to be out ahead of the crowd. Max paused to give a stack of wooden crates strung with chicken wire a thorough sniff. They were explorers. The scouts sent out to identify potential dangers.

Jake kept his head down as they moved through the cages containing birds designated as "broilers," a large variety of ducks and some rather noisy geese. They made it to the last row, which held an impressive array of turkeys and guinea fowl. He was about to call Max back to him when the dog suddenly dropped to his rump and barked three times, his attention locked on an oversize plastic storage container shoved under a folding table.

Reaching for his police radio, he made his way closer. "Canine ID'd device. Poultry Barn." He reattached Max's lead and coaxed the dog into taking a few steps back. Without taking his eyes off the tub, he gave Max's ears a scratch. "Good dog."

Max shifted closer to his leg, but the two of them continued to stare transfixed until Cass's voice yanked him out of his trance. But she wasn't talking to him. She was reminding Bud Thompson to check the small cages and pens that housed the petting animals beyond the entertainment area dedicated to entertaining the fair's smaller patrons.

The brusque exchange of orders and information washed over him like a wave. Of all the people in the world, Cassidy Walker was here. And so was shot at a second chance. Maybe.

If he could figure out the right words to say to get Cass to forgive him.

"Donovan?"

Jake shook himself like Max after a bath. The radio gripped in his hand, he took a moment to clear his mind before he answered. "Go ahead, Chief."

"Leave a marker at the area then move on to the next building. I'll send a team over."

"Ten-four." He unzipped another compartment on his vest and pulled out a yellow plastic square. Shaking open the evidence marker so it stood like a tent, he placed it on top of the folding table. "Yellow marker Number 01 placed at the southeast corner of the building. There's a table with a storage container shoved beneath. The storage tub is our mark."

"Copy," the lead investigator responded. "Noted. Move on."

"Yes, sir."

Jake gave Max another pat and a small bit of treat to reward his hard work. "Let's run through the rabbits, then we'll get you another drink and something to eat." The two of them jogged down the hill to the building situated between the poultry and the main concourse. "Good thing you're not the type to go chasing bunnies," he said as he let Max off his leash at the door.

Ten minutes later, they were moving on. "Rabbit Barn is clear," he informed the team.

"Disposal moving to Poultry now." Aronson paused. "I have people in the horse barns. Head to Goats and Sheep and then the swine."

"Copy."

Jake waved to the team assembling outside the Poultry Barn, then turned to jog downhill. They passed the horse stable and the show ring, their steps slowing as they approached the building on far west side of the fairgrounds. On impulse, he grabbed Cass's radio and spoke into it.

"I don't suppose it's a coincidence the sheep, swine and poultry are kept away from the main drag."

Cass didn't disappoint. "If fairgoers want to experience the stinkier species, they know where to find them."

"It's hard to believe horses and cows are deemed the better option," he countered.

"Where are you? Obviously not Goats and Sheep or Swine barns."

"Yet," he added. "We found one at Poultry, nothing at Rabbits."

"So, we're up to seven."

She started to say more, but he cut her off when another call came through on the official channel. "Number eight is in Cattle Barn 1."

"We're getting close," Cass said, her voice a mix of tension and hopefulness. There was a pause and then she spoke softly. "It's almost two, Jake. Don't go in there yet."

"I'll remind the others to fall back for a few minutes." He turned in the direction of the midway. Jake checked his watch. It was four minutes to the hour. He called to base. "Top of the hour. Should we take ten, Chief?"

A moment later, Aronson replied. "Yeah, everyone fall back until five past."

Without giving it much thought, Jake clicked his tongue and he and Max headed for the midway. When they arrived at the carousel, they found Cass sitting slumped against a glittery green seahorse, her expression a heart-wrenching mix of loneliness and determination. She whirled past, her attention fixed on the bench across from her.

"Hey."

Her head popped up. "Oh. Hey. You came back."

Trying to play it cool even though his heart raced as he and Max hopped onto the moving platform, he shrugged. "We're taking ten to clear the top of the hour."

She nodded, pressing her lips together as she took the information in. "Aronson must have a lot of faith in your word if he's agreed to pause the hunt based on a hunch."

"I think he has faith in our combined theory." He pulled a collapsable water bowl from Max's vest and shook it open. Cracking the cap on a bottle of water, he dumped half of it into the bowl before taking a long pull of what was left for himself. "Besides, it's the only one we've got so far."

Cass checked the display on her phone. "One fifty-nine."

Her voice was tense. Jake wished there was something he could say to ease her anxiety, but he knew anything he attempted would sound trite. It was clear the person behind all this was targeting Cass, and there was no way to make her feel better about any of it. But he felt compelled to try. He opened his mouth to speak but snapped it shut again when Max straightened abruptly then plunked his big muzzle down on Cass's leg.

"Oh!" she gasped in surprise.

"Max," Jake said, a note of reprimand in his tone.

But the shepherd didn't budge. Instead, he looked up at Cass, large ears twitching and amber eyes sincere.

"Sweet boy," she cooed, resting her hand on the dog's head.

Jake stared at his partner, lips parted in surprise. Max was a good dog. An obedient dog. A well-trained and enthusiastic officer at work, and an easy companion with him. But Jake never referred to Max as a sweet boy. Sure, he was friendly and even a little affectionate toward Jake, but Max was extremely task-oriented. He worked, ate, ran and slept. Bred to be a K-9 officer, usually Max barely acknowledged any human other than Jake.

"Wow," Jake managed to say at last.

Cass tilted her head, her hair falling to the side as she eyed him curiously. "What?"

"He doesn't…" Stopping to clear the croak from his throat, he gave a short chuckle. "I've never seen him do that."

"No?" She turned her full attention to Max. "Maybe he's not

into you," she teased, gracing his partner with a warm, conspiratorial smile. "Maybe he's a ladies' man…dog," she crooned, wrinkling her nose at Max as she beamed approval at him.

For the first time since Max had sprung from his trainer's kennel, Jake felt a pang of jealousy. The problem was, he didn't know if he was envious of Cass's easy manner with Max, or the fact she'd looked at Max the same way she used to look at him.

Like he was…everything.

His mind flashed to the last weekend he and Cass had spent together. The transition from high school to college had been tough. The three hours between them feeling endless. Their phone calls stretched into the nights, but often they'd end up bickering more than talking. In a desperate attempt to get back on the same page, he'd come down from Fayetteville for the weekend, and they'd come here. To the fair.

They'd eaten their fill of fried food, ridden every ride, and even played a few of the rigged games. On the surface, it had felt like a good day, but something was off. Cass was distant. Standoffish. She hadn't smiled at him, like once, the whole time they'd been together. And then he'd heard she'd been spending time with a classmate who'd attended their high school—a guy Jake knew for a fact had always liked Cass—and he'd decided to cut and run before she decided to dump him.

"Jake?"

Her voice jolted him from his reverie. "Huh?"

"It's two minutes past two." She spoke so softly it was almost a whisper.

As if remembering his dignity, Max lifted his chin from her knee and stretched out on his stomach between them. Jake glanced down at his dog then up at her. Their eyes met, and she offered him a tremulous little smile. Her eyes shone with hope, but his stomach filled with dread.

This moment felt so much like day at the fair so long ago. Jake remembered wanting everything to be right and easy between them. To feel the way they used to feel. Without doubts or questions. Then Cassidy spoke the two worst words in the English language out loud.

"What if—"

But she didn't get to complete the thought before her phone buzzed with an incoming message.

Have your pals been messing with the presents I left for you, Lieutenant?

She held the phone out for Jake to see. "I'm guessing the pirate ship was supposed to be two o'clock."

"Maybe so." Jake radioed Aronson. "Another message. Looks like we preempted the pyrotechnics planned for two o'clock."

A faint cheer rose from the far side of the carnival. Jake stood and was about to turn to leave when Cass called him back. "Wait! Look." She thrust the phone at him again. This time, the person on the other end hadn't bothered to make a new thread.

You want to speed up the timeline? Fine by me.

He opened his mouth to question the meaning of the message but his words were drowned out by a substantial blast. The explosion made everything around them shudder and shake.

"Oh, no," Cass moaned, rising to her feet. She pressed one hand to her mouth as she gripped the seahorse's head for balance.

An eerie moment of silence swallowed the first burst of commotion. Then a jumble of voices on both radios broke through. A plume of smoke rose from the direction of the livestock barns. The warning blip of an emergency vehicle siren sliced through the mayhem. He caught the words "Cattle Barn" loud and clear.

Jake glanced over his shoulder. "I'll be right back."

But Cass turned back to the bench where she'd left her own radio. He and Max hopped off the ride and ran halfway across the concourse when he caught sight of an ambulance parked on the hill outside Cattle Barn 4.

He broke into a jog, Max loping along easily at his side. When they rounded the open doors at the back of the ambulance, Jake spotted Sergeant Winter seated on the metal deck, a blood-soaked wad of cloth in his hand. An EMS tech was working on closing a wound on his cheek with a butterfly bandage.

"How are your guys?"

"They're fine. We were heading back in when it blew. I didn't hit the dirt fast enough. Caught a big splinter," Winter reported.

Jake turned to look at the gaping hole where the massive cow had stood a short time before. A bevy of first responders tended to the blast site while what appeared to be the entire fair security team did their best to move some freaked-out cattle from the other end of the building.

Cass's voice came across the channel she and her team kept open, and he stepped away from the commotion to better hear her. But she wasn't speaking to him. Instead, she was barking orders to her own team.

"Bud, get me a phone I can use and the name and number for whoever is in charge at the Air Force Base. We need to get some records pulled."

Jake allowed himself a grim smile. Cassidy Walker was done being a pawn in whatever game this joker thought they were playing. It was game on.

Chapter Seven

Cassidy watched Jake Donovan walk away from her. Again.

The gnawing ache caused by his sudden absence in her life had abated over the years, yet seeing him again made it clear it had never gone away entirely. But she couldn't let herself go there again. Not when there was so much at stake. Maybe not ever.

They were still kids when their lives veered off in different directions. Jake had been determined to attend the university in Fayetteville once they graduated and was excited to live the full college experience. But her family struggled to send her as far as Little Rock. While he was going to football games and meeting people from all over, she was working at a sandwich shop every hour she wasn't in class. After a few months, the distance between campuses and the differences in their life-styles proved to be too much.

When Jake had told her he thought they should call things off, she'd slumped into a mild depression. Her mother was the one who'd talked her back to the land of the living. She'd made Cassidy promise to visit the campus health center and speak to one of the counselors. The counselor had, in turn, encouraged her to find her own purpose in life.

But the breakup left her reeling emotionally and struggling to focus in school.

She'd begun speaking to a young woman in her English Lit-erature section who was a member of the ROTC. For the first time, Cass had considered doing something other than the expected four years of college.

She'd stayed in school but switched her major from Business Management to Criminal Justice. Then she'd joined an officer training program.

Until today, Cassidy always considered her service the best decision she'd ever made.

Now someone was making her question her choices.

She'd spoken to Bud and put a plan in motion, but now she had to make sure everyone was on the same page. Cassidy flagged down the fire trainee who'd been checking on her periodically. "Hey," she shouted, cupping her hands around her mouth to make her voice carry. "Hey, T.B.?"

The guy looked up and she beckoned him to her. "Ma'am?"

Clinging to one of the poles at the edge of the platform, she spoke in short, clear sentences, pausing each time the ride circled around to the back of the midway.

"Would you ask Colonel Aronson to come see me? Tell him it's important. I have information that might pertain to our bomber."

"Yes, ma'am." The firefighter gave a short sharp nod and turned away.

Cassidy watched as her messenger trotted up the hill toward the arena.

She was going to have to ask for help. Not something at the top of her skill set. But if she could get what she wanted from the base, she would have a boatload of information to sift through. Even if they could get a laptop or tablet to her, Cassidy didn't think she could focus on a screen for more than a few seconds without getting sick. And if she was going to make any sense of the data, she needed someone who could seek out patterns.

Feeling slightly dejected, she made her way over to the bench and sat heavily. The bulk of the pack forced her to bounce off the back of the seat. "Stupid backpack. Stupid Cassidy."

But even as she chastised herself she knew she didn't mean it.

The bomber was right. There was no way she would have let that big-eyed boy wear what might be an incendiary device on his shoulders.

She slanted her head back and stared at the carousel's canopy. The paint was flaking and peeling in spots. She'd be sure to mention it to the manager of the attractions company they'd contracted. Not that they'd care. She'd pointed out a few places where the facades of the games and rides had looked a little worse for wear when they'd done their safety inspection, but the man had always seemed to be in a hurry to be elsewhere.

She could almost hear him now saying nobody ever looked up when riding a carousel. And he was probably right under normal circumstances. She conceded the point in the argument with herself but didn't mean proper maintenance could be skipped.

"Ms. Walker? You wanted to see me?"

She glanced over and saw Colonel Aronson approaching. He was a tall man with a well-worn face and a no-nonsense demeanor. The colonel stopped off to side of the carousel and planted himself with his feet spread wide and arms clasped behind his back.

Cassidy smiled when she realized he was standing in a Parade Rest stance. "Did you serve, Colonel?" she shouted as she whirled past.

Aronson didn't answer right away, but the next time she came around, he gave a brief nod and said, "US Marine Corps, ma'am."

"USAF," she called back to him as she took a ride around the back once again.

"So I hear," he replied. "What can I do for you?"

Cassidy quickly surmised that the site commander had no intention of hopping onto her merry-go-round of torture, so she came quickly to the point on her pass.

"I need to put a call in to the base at Jacksonville. I was in the Security Forces there when on active duty." She completed another circuit, but the second he came into sight it again she began speaking. "Some of the messages I've received make it clear whoever's doing this knows about my service." She had to wait for another circuit to pass. "They likely know my assigned duties. As you can imagine, Military Police aren't terribly popular."

Aronson nodded some more. "Concur," he said as she circled around again.

Cassidy swallowed her annoyance at the man's taciturn conversational style. After all, he was the one up there trying to direct teams ready to defuse bombs when she was simply sitting on one.

"I'm going to need help sifting through the data. If I can get someone," she amended. "Reading isn't easy up here."

"I can imagine. I'll see what I can do."

She winced as she forced the next part out. "I may also need some weight thrown behind my request."

Aronson straightened. "I think you could ask the governor for about anything right now, ma'am."

She gestured to her mobile phone and then tapped the magnetic battery pack attached to the back of it. "We can only assume my phone is compromised. Bud Thompson is supposed to be bringing me another, but I'd like to get this moving as quickly as possible." She paused, looking for any sign of compliance. When he continued to return her stare, she knew she would have to be more direct with her request. "Would you put the call in?"

The colonel frowned in confusion. "To the governor, or to the base?"

"Both. Either. I think the request would have more heft coming from you, sir."

"I don't know anything about how they run things at the base," he told her.

"Listen, I know our best offense is a good defense, and all, but I believe we should take some action. We can't sit here and wait for things to play out on this joker's timeline."

By the time she came around again, Aronson had moved closer to the ride. "I agree with you. I'll put in a call to the governor's office and see if someone will reach out to the base commander. I can also get somebody from our Cyber Crime Division to help look for patterns in whatever data you can get from the base."

"Thank you, sir."

"You're doing great, Ms. Walker." Aronson began to back away, but before he cleared the security fencing, he turned. "Hey, since we're asking favors… When you see Donovan next, would you remind him he reports to me and not you?"

Cassidy spluttered a laugh. "Yes, sir. I certainly will."

He touched a finger to the edge of his helmet in a small salute. "We'll get you out of this," he assured her.

The moment he turned away, Cassidy stretched out on her side, facing the back of the bench, but she couldn't maintain the position for long. Oddly enough, she found it harder to fight off the nausea when she couldn't track where she was in the circuit.

Gripping the edge of the bench, she pushed up and twisted her body until she could take the same position but facing outward. She locked in on chip in the bench across from her and focused on sorting the possibilities.

Number one, if it was somebody from her Air Force days, it would somewhat certainly be someone who considered her more foe than friend. Military Police or Security Forces—it didn't matter what you called them—the people charged with the duty of keeping other people in line were never the most sought-after friends.

Sure, she'd made some good connections with colleagues. More after she'd moved from patrol to training duties. As a trainer, her fellow officers had viewed her more as a teacher than as a cop. Regardless, she'd absolutely made more enemies in her years of service than pals. It was the nature of the beast.

That brought her to point number two. The supposition that whoever was doing this felt they had a score to settle with her. It was clearly someone who thought they knew her well. At least well enough to make assumptions. She could probably eliminate servicemen and women she'd encountered in more mundane circumstances such as traffic checkpoints or dealing with identification issues. Most of the day-to-day misdemeanors were unlikely as well. Drunk and disorderly conduct arrests we're a dime a dozen. Plus, the people she'd busted in those cases were usually angrier with whoever had ratted them out than with her.

This was likely somebody she'd encountered under more serious circumstances. She'd made numerous arrests in her career. Many of them significant crimes. Was the person who was doing this the perpetrator of her twelfth arrest? The twelfth overall, or that resulted in a felony conviction? Was the "dozen" part significant, or was she overly fixated on the number twelve?

She pondered all the possibilities, weighing each one carefully. They each had pros and cons, but none felt quite right. Cassidy's gut told her she was on the right track when it came to major infractions versus minor. But minor transgressions could also become major quickly if they piled up on top of one another.

She was startled from her rumination by the clatter of toenails on metal. A cool, damp muscle inserted itself into her ear.

Max was back. Jake was here.

"Hey now, player," she said, laughing as she heaved herself into a sitting position again. Looking down at the somber-eyed dog, she smiled. "I don't think we know each other well enough for those kinds of greetings, Max."

"He's not great with boundaries," Jackson quipped, playing along with her teaching tone. "I keep telling him curiosity is for cats, but he doesn't believe me." At the mention of felines, Max tipped his head to the side and eyed his partner skeptically. Jake grimaced. "He's not the biggest fan of c-a-t-s."

"Really?" She found herself genuinely curiously intrigued. "I always thought that was a myth."

"I don't think he wishes them any ill. He's simply baffled by their existence."

"Ah, I see," Cassidy said, nodding slowly then reaching out to pet the side of the dog's neck. "I feel the same way about a lot of people." Tipping her chin up, she eyed Jake warily. "Anyone hurt?"

He shook his head. "A couple of cuts from flying debris, but nothing serious."

"Jake, I think we need to talk about whether these devices should be disarmed or not."

Much to her surprise, he nodded. "I was thinking the same thing."

"You were?"

"But we might be too late," he conceded. "They're already ticked we messed with their timeline, and considering they expended two of the devices of their own volition, I have to think we can't put too much stock in them holding the line with the rest. They've proven they're willing to pivot when they need to."

"Agreed," Cassidy said with a sharp bob of her head. "Colonel Aronson came down and spoke with me. He's going to ask the governor's office to forward my request for information from Little Rock Air Force Base. The colonel also asked me to remind you report to him and not me." She arched an eyebrow. "Have you been neglecting your chain of command?"

Jake sucked air in between his teeth, but two spots of color rose in his cheeks. "Yeah, I need to run up there and get his feedback on the timeline situation."

She fixed him with a patient stare. "You don't need to keep checking on me, Jake."

"Says you."

Cassidy's heart leaped and then flipped in her chest. What was that supposed to mean? She didn't dare ask. "I have a really nice probationary firefighter hanging around," she said with an airy wave. "Go check in. Do what you need to do."

"I will," he assured her, but the stubborn tilt of his chin said something entirely different.

"I'm waiting for Bud to bring me a phone. I'll reach out to the base as well. Try to light a fire under them. But not literally," she added.

At last, Jake looked directly at her, but when their eyes met, her breath tangled in her throat. The stark fear she spotted in his eyes sent a chill down her spine.

"What is it?"

He shook his head as if he was still trying to wrap his mind around their current circumstances. "Whoever this is isn't messing around, Cass. The device at the cattle barn packed a wallop. I didn't stick around in the poultry house long enough to assess whatever was hidden in storage container, but I have a feeling we're dealing with somebody who knows explosives well."

"I agree. It's someone with experience in building and detonating bombs or IEDs. Or an electronics expert who spends too much time on YouTube," she added dryly.

Jake picked up the thread. "There was a sort of timeline suggested in the beginning, but we know they can detonate them remotely. Because they are surveilling the scene and have the capability to change the game on a whim, it makes locating and disabling devices more of a risk."

She pondered the possibilities. "I think we're better off assuming it's somebody with a military background," she said. "I know there's a lot out on the internet these days, but I'm also going with the assumption it's somebody with real training. Possibly someone I arrested during my time with Security Forces."

"Sounds plausible."

Cassidy should have felt a modicum of vindication in having her theory confirmed by another member of law enforcement, but at this juncture, she doubted anything was going to make her feel better. "I don't want anyone else to get hurt, Jake."

"No one wants anyone to get hurt, but we all know the risks when we sign up for this job."

"I don't want my past to be the reason someone has their future stolen from them," she insisted, a visceral need to voice her deepest, darkest fear pushing the words out of her.

Jake scowled then gave a tight nod. "I'm going to check in with Aronson. Then I think the three of us need to put our heads together to figure out next steps."

Twenty minutes later, the two men sat on the bench across from her, Max stretched out at their feet.

"I think we're agreed." Colonel Aronson sat back, his expression grim. "I'll speak to the other team leads, and we'll prioritize locating the remaining devices, but hold off on disarming."

Cassidy leaned in. "But you'll hold your people back and let three o'clock go, right?"

They exchanged uneasy glances. Letting a bomb blow went against everything they worked for, but Aronson agreed. They needed to let the perp think they were still flailing. Because they were.

"As long as your people can live with the collateral damage," the commander said, his tone resigned.

"I'll make sure it's okay," she assured him. "We need to buy some time."

Aronson stood. "I'll make sure we pull back to a neutral site from ten minutes to the hour to ten after. If nothing blows, we'll reevaluate the window."

The phone Bud Thompson provided lit up with an incoming call. The on-screen ID showed the call to be coming from the Little Rock Air Force Base.

"It's the base." She swiped to connect the call.

Aronson turned to Jake. "I'm hopping off. Keep me in the loop."

"Hello?" Cassidy watched as Aronson jumped down, then put the call on speakerphone so Jake could listen in.

"This is Colonel Vesta Linton. Commander, 19th Mission Support Group. Is this *the* Cassidy Walker?" The caller's question carried a teasing note.

Cassidy couldn't help but smile as she put the pieces together. "Vesta? Holy cow." She laughed. "Who let you be in charge?"

"Shh. They haven't figured it out." Colonel Linton sounded as warm and friendly as Cass remembered. She was also a woman who didn't waste much time on pleasantries. "I would say I'm surprised to hear from you after so long, but not nearly as surprised as I was to hear from Governor Beauford's office. Girl, what have you gotten yourself into?"

Her smile stretched wide, but then she caught Jake's quizzical expression, and it quickly faded. "Vesta, I've got Jake Donovan from the State Police here with me, and we have you on speaker."

"Understood."

Cassidy glanced at Jake, then dove in. "We have a nasty situation here, and we need your help."

Vesta Linton shifted into business mode without hesitation. "Fill me in."

"There's a person claiming to have planted multiple explosive devices around the state fairgrounds."

"The fairgrounds? Didn't the fair open this week?" she responded without missing a beat.

"Tomorrow." Cassidy forced the bile rising in her throat down, then continued. "Possibly."

Vesta didn't miss a beat. "What can I do for you?"

Blowing out a breath that ruffled her hair, she elaborated.

"We think this may be someone with a vendetta. One maybe connected to my time on the base."

"They're coming after you personally?"

"Sounds like it." Cassidy's tone was grim.

"What do you need from me?"

"Records," she responded, meeting Jake's eyes directly. "Anyone I tagged while I was there. We're going to be taking a hard look at any of the more serious cases, but if you can dump everything into a file, we can parse it. There will be a tech from the State Police reaching out to you."

"How much information? There may be limits to what I can give you," Vesta warned.

"Let's start with serial number, date, charges and any sentence imposed," Cassidy said, holding Jake's wrist as she rattled the request off. "If we can find some kind of pattern, we might ask you to go deeper."

Vesta hummed her agreement. "Fair enough. Who should I be looking to hear from?"

Jake leaned over to speak into the phone. "Special Agent Emma Parker, from our Cyber Crime Division, will be reaching out."

"Very good," Vesta replied. "I'll get the information pulled. Cassidy. I expect to hear from you when this situation is cleared up."

"Will do, Vesta. Thank you." Cassidy ended the call and found Jake watching her, a curious expression on his face. "What?"

"Old friend?"

"Actually, yes." She matched his tone but didn't offer anything more.

Jake didn't give up. "You serve together?"

Cassidy sighed and then fixed him with a bland stare. "Yes. Actually, Vesta was a member of my first training class."

His eyebrows shot skyward. "And now she's in charge?"

"Looks that way," she said, going for a casual tone.

But Jake was not accepting the brush-off. He bent closer, a mischievous gleam in his eye. "Did she get promoted over you? Is that why you left?"

"You've been watching too many daytime dramas," she said with a laugh.

His smile came slow. "Do they even have those anymore?"

"I bet you listen to true crime podcasts while you cruise around with your doggo."

Jake chuckled, then made a move to stand. "Max prefers classic rock on satellite radio."

Cassidy's heart sank as she watched Max scramble to his feet as well. They were heading back into the search, and once again, she'd be left alone with only her own personal bomb for company.

"Hey, don't forget to update your boss."

Jake swiveled and gave her a smart salute. "Will do." Then, walking backward, he checked his watch. "We'll be back for three o'clock. We'll bring water and snacks."

A glance at her own phone sent a surge of relief through her. Twenty minutes. She'd see them again in twenty more minutes.

"Something salty," she requested. "Like me."

He held up a hand to indicate message received. "Sweet it is."

Before she could answer, he turned and jogged away.

Cassidy sagged in her seat, but smiled nonetheless. Jake Donovan thought she was sweet. It wasn't much, but it was enough. For now.

Chapter Eight

Tensions on the concourse of Barton Coliseum ran high. Colonel Aronson was in deep discussion with two other men. One was dressed in field gear, the other in a suit. The shorter one turned and Jake spotted the Little Rock Fire Department insignia on his shirt. He could only assume the other was city police.

Evan Furst and another firefighter hung back, close enough to catch the tenor of the conversation if not the details. "What's going on?" Jake drew Max to a halt beside them.

"Ain't nobody happy," the man beside Furst grumbled. He shot Jake a sidelong glance as he disengaged. "I'll be outside if anyone's looking for me."

Jake watched him go, idly wondering how he'd managed to step on the guy's toes when they'd never crossed paths. Turning back to Furst, he cocked a brow. "What did that mean?"

The firefighter shrugged. "The teams aren't pleased with the decision not to disarm."

Jake instantly understood the mild animosity was directed toward him. No doubt word had spread he'd been involved in the decision to let things ride until they came up with a better angle. "Ah. I see."

"I guess your girlfriend on the carousel is the one calling the shots," Furst said, crossing his arms over his chest as if settling in for the confrontation.

"A—she's not my girlfriend." He was extra careful to leave the "anymore" echoing around in his head off the end of the statement. "B—this literally is her circus and she has this creep's monkey strapped to her back, so I think it's reasonable to heed her input. And C—if anyone is going to be responsible for the property damage or delay to the opening, it's her and not us."

Furst's shoulders dropped slightly, but his jaw remained tight. "Sitting back and letting things blow is not what we do."

"Rushing in when we know we can't predict the pattern or understand the perpetrator's motivation would be reckless. We know he can detonate at will, and we know he has eyes on us," Jake countered. "As long as the price of holding off is repairing a few buildings rather than paying a condolence call to a team member's family, I think it's the right course of action."

"Course of inaction," Furst replied.

Tiring of the circular discussion, Jake jerked his chin at the man in the suit. "Who's the tie?"

"Governor's office." Furst cracked a wry half smile. "Skittish as a drop of water in a hot skillet."

Jake chuckled at the description, then glanced back at the doors. "We'll I'm not going to wade into those waters." He clicked his tongue and Max was on his feet again, ready to go. "We're heading for the Swine and Sheep barns."

"Hope you brought nose plugs," Furst called after them.

Hitting the crash bar on the tinted-glass door, Jake blinked as they emerged into the bright sunlight once again. Aronson might have different orders for him now the game had changed, but the last thing he wanted was to be ensnared in command debates. He'd been lucky the colonel was willing to listen to the line of reasoning he and Cass had laid out, and now the guy was taking heat for it. The best thing Jake could do for his own career was to put as much distance between himself and the decision-makers as possible.

Other than the Equestrian Center, the Goats and Sheep, and

Swine barns were about as far as he could get without leaving the fairgrounds.

"Come on, boy."

He and Max walked down the hill at a brisk pace. Jake looked from side to side, but did not stop as they passed Cattle Barn 3. He slowed at the opening of Cattle 4 and his gut clenched when he spotted the splintered wood and straw bedding blown past the entrance.

Sergeant Winter sat sideways in the driver's seat of the cart they'd been using, a bandage on his cheek and his phone pressed to his ear. He raised a hand in acknowledgment when Jake and Max passed, but he didn't make any move to intercept them.

Jake wondered idly where Winter's team was but didn't dwell on it. No doubt Aronson had redistributed them and left Winter to babysit the site on the off chance the bomber might wander through to inspect their handiwork.

He exchanged wordless waves with a couple of other teams as they took the long way around one of the horse barns. The grassy patch outside the Swine Barn was dotted with signs listing judging times and a few sponsor advertisements utilizing the traditional hog call heard at Arkansas Razorbacks events— Wooo, Pig, Sooie!—to their best advantage.

The smell emanating from the barn set Max's nose twitching, but Jake couldn't help but grimace. "Phew, pig," he said, wrinkling his nose.

"Sooie for sure," came the disembodied answer from another stall.

Letting Max take the lead, Jake came around the corner and found one of the Little Rock PD tactical team members engaged in a staring contest with a 250-pound spotted hog.

"Whoa."

"Says his name is Wilbur," the officer said dryly.

Jake nodded a greeting. "Hello, Wilbur."

"You must be a mind reader," the other man said, his drawl soft around the edges.

"How so?"

"We were about to call for a sniffer," he said, nodding down at Max. He hitched his belt higher, then jerked a thumb over his shoulder. "Got a mystery bag. A duffel. Down at the end, not inside a stall."

Jake raised his eyebrows, then checked his watch. It was a quarter to three already. Time was moving way too fast.

"Why don't you guys fall back, and I'll let Max check it out before we're pulled out for the top of the hour."

The officer snorted indelicately. "This is the craziest darn thing I've ever seen." Running his hand down the front of his vest, he shrugged. "Sure. Have at it." He stepped around Jake and Max, then called to the other side of the barn, "K-9 on site. Let's move on, y'all."

Jake waited until two officers emerged from the far aisle, then asked, "Where's the bag?"

The man who'd greeted them smirked. "Won't your doggie find it on his own?"

"Where's the bag?" Jake let his impatience seep into his tone.

One of the other officers pointed to the opposite end of the barn. "Inside the entrance. Looks like it was placed there intentionally. Not tossed or left behind," he added. He held his hands up defensively as the others turned to glare at him. "What? I want to get this over with and go home."

"Don't we all?" Jake bent to unclip Max's lead. "There you go, Max. As the nice man said, have at it."

Max took off, his nose to the ground, the fur along the ridge of his back rippling. Jake could tell by the dog's intense concentration he'd already caught a whiff of something. He followed in his partner's wake, waiting for a positive identification.

It didn't take long.

As the call went out for them to fall back, Max sat down at

the end of the row and stared at a bag parked inside the cinder-block wall and barked the confirmation.

"Good boy." Jake squatted beside Max and eyed the bag.

The duffel was the kind used to carry a change of clothes to the gym. Small, well-worn and made of faded navy-blue nylon. Jake couldn't spot a logo or any kind of branding. If there was a manufacturer's tag inside, it would be someone else's job to get to it.

"Let's go." He stepped toward the door closest to them and pushed out into the gathering afternoon heat. He secured Max's lead then relayed the location of the bomb. "We have a positive on the Swine Barn," he said into his radio. "North end of the building, duffel bag inside the door to the left, up against a wall."

"Ten-four," Aronson said. "Now get out of there."

"We're out." He took a deep breath of fresh air, then expelled it slowly. The midway started beyond the barn, and though he'd received the colonel's message about his chain of command loud and clear, Jake found himself cutting a direct path to the carousel.

When he hopped onto the ride, he found Cass seated on her seahorse bench, the wrapper of a fully-loaded sub sandwich spread across her lap. She looked up at their approach, her check stuffed. "Suddenly, I'm starving," she mumbled as she chewed.

Jake froze in place, watching as she dabbed at her mouth with a paper napkin, heat crawling up his neck. "Sorry," he said, his voice cracking like a teenager's. He cleared his throat. "Where'd you get that?"

"My pal T.B. brought it to me." She opened a bottle of water and took a long pull. "Anything happening?"

"We ID'd one before the call went out to fall back and I came straight here."

Cass lowered the sandwich to the wrapper. "Where was it?"

"Swine Barn."

She raised a thumb to her mouth and licked a bit of mayo from the side. "Gives us eight."

"Nine."

"The gate, Manny's food stand, Cattle 1 and 4, Poultry…" She trailed off, searching her memory as she counted on her fingers.

"Arkansas Building, pirate ride and Swine," he finished.

She held up her fingers. "Right. Eight."

He inclined his head in her direction. "Backpack."

Cass wet her lips. The nervous tic combined with the widening of her eyes to give him a glimpse of the girl he'd known so well. It was all Jake could do to keep from grabbing her and holding her close.

Let the jerk who was doing this to her blow them both sky-high.

"I keep forgetting about the backpack," she confessed, reeling him back from his daydream.

"I can't think about anything else."

She broke eye contact, returning her attention to the sandwich in her lap. She picked up the half she'd started on, then spoke without looking directly at him. "Want half? I doubt I can eat all of this."

Jake's stomach growled an affirmative, and he took the seat across from her. "Sure."

She wrapped a napkin around the uneaten half and offered it to him. Max's hopeful gaze followed her every movement. Jake lowered his hand and said, "Down."

The dog stretched out between their feet, resting his muzzle on his paws and shamelessly working her over with nothing but his expressive eyebrows. "Poor guy," she cooed. "I'd share mine, but I bet the mean man won't let me."

"The mean man is responsible for keeping his partner as healthy as possible," Jake said without rancor. "If I fell prey to puppy-dog eyes, this beast would weigh over a hundred pounds, easy."

Cass chuckled as she chewed. "But he has such handsome puppy-dog eyes." She beamed at her new best friend. "Tell me about the Swine Barn."

Jake shrugged and sat back. "Not much to tell. The team found a duffel bag. Max confirmed the presence of explosives, but we had to back off before anyone could take a closer look."

"Colonel Aronson told me your computer whiz got the file Vesta sent with information on the arrests I made," she informed him. "They're supposed to let me know if they have any questions or find a pattern."

"Let's hope they find a thread we can tug."

"I hate thinking this is all connected to my past." She gave a sort of laugh-snort, then shook her head ruefully. "I don't even feel like I have a past, you know? All I've done is go from school to the service, and then to work."

"No disgruntled exes?"

The question came out before he could check himself. The last thing he wanted to hear about was her love life. The only comfort he could take was in knowing she wasn't about to start singing the praises of their old classmate, Robby McAvoy. Whatever they'd had going in college must have fizzled out quickly, Jake assumed. Last he'd heard, Robby was married to someone else.

"I don't know, you tell me," she said, arching her eyebrows and fixing him with a pointed stare. "How disgruntled can a guy be if he's the one who did the breaking up?"

"Depends—"

But Jake didn't get to finish his thought.

A flash followed by an ear-splitting bang that went off way too close. Everything around them shuddered. Max let out a sharp yip when Jake yanked Cass off the bench, covering both of their bodies with his. The remnants of their half-eaten sandwiches littered the floor. Jake found himself staring at a piece of cheese dangling from the edge of the bench where she'd sat. A dozen dull blows rained down on his back. Like someone was pelting them with tennis balls. He lifted his head enough to peer out, but they were at the back of the ride, away from the fallout.

By the time they came around to the concourse again, the initial tremor was offset by a rush of footfalls. He turned his head and something yellow rolled out from under the bench.

Max growled, deep and menacing.

Cass panted, then pushed against him. "Let me up. I'm squishing poor Max."

Jake eased off enough for her to push up but did not pull back enough for her to rise. Not until he could wrap his head around what had happened. Max growled again, and Jake forced himself to focus on what the dog might be warning them about. Following the line of the shepherd's snout, he spotted the yellow orb rocking listlessly on the metal platform.

It wasn't a tennis ball. It was a rubber duck.

Cassidy fit the puzzle pieces together first. Pointing to a spot at the center of the stuffed-animal-strewn midway, she said, "I think they blew up the duck pond game." She slid back onto the bench, battling her hair back from her face with impatient swats. "That's six."

"What? No. It's number ten," he corrected, catching hold of a nearby pole to steady himself.

She shook her head; her forehead puckered in concentration. "No, six blown," she says, sounding a bit breathless. "They've detained half the devices."

"Oh. Yeah." Jake nodded as he surveyed the chaotic scene, every muscle in his body tensed in an effort to hold back. All he wanted to do was hop off this infernal ride and run over to help. They needed to put a stop to all this. Sooner rather than later. "You're right. But we've identified another four."

"Only two more to go," she said with a decisive nod. Cass

tilted her head in the direction of the assembled emergency workers. "Go find out how bad it is and if anyone was hurt. Give me your map and I'll try to pinpoint some other likely locations."

Jake unzipped the pocket on his vest and pulled out the crumpled map he'd been marking with each new discovery. "I haven't had a chance to circle the Swine Barn," he said as he handed it over.

She groped around in the crevice of the bench for the pen someone had brought to her. "I'll do it. Go. Let me know what's happening."

Jake glanced down at his partner. "Max, stay."

"You don't… I don't need a guard dog."

"He stays with you," he said without looking back. "I'll only be a minute." When he glanced down, he was surprised to find a bright yellow rubber duck clutched in his fist. The second he opened his fingers, the duck drew a deep squawk of a breath. "Here. Catch."

Reflexes quick as a cat, Cass snagged the duck he lobbed to her from the air. To his surprise, she peeked at the bottom of the toy, then showed him the bright blue dot. "You picked a winner."

"Everything's coming up aces." He jumped down. "Back in a sec."

"Don't forget to pick out your prize," she reminded him.

Jake shook his head as he jogged away. Cassidy was crooning and cooing at the dog. When he looked back, he found Max gazing up at her adoringly, clearly enjoying the attention. Again, Jake pushed down the sharp spike of envy jabbing his gut.

"I am not jealous of a dog."

Still, he couldn't blame Max for being smitten by a beautiful woman lavishing attention on him. His dog had lived the bachelor life alongside Jake in the years since he'd come to live with him. Oh, the dog trainer they worked with was a woman.

And Jake dated every now and again, but he honestly could not remember the last time he'd brought a date back to his place.

"Hey, Donovan," someone shouted as he approached.

Craning his neck, he spotted Evan Furst standing off to the side of the crowd, a small white rectangle in his hand. He made his way over to the man, sweeping the scene as he stepped carefully through the mess of splintered wood, chunks of filler from prizes blown apart by the blast, and ducks scattered in the stream of water left from the obliterated pond.

"Hey," he said as he approached the firefighter. "Anyone hurt?"

Furst shook his head. "Only the ducks."

"Threw some as far as the carousel. I drew a blue one," he said with a wry smile. "Not sure how big a prize that gets me."

Evan gestured to the dozens of dismembered, sodden or smoldering carnival prizes scattered around them. "I think you can take your pick."

Jake jerked his chin at the card in the other man's hand. "What do you have there?"

"Could be nothing," Furst said, frowning at the card then turning it around for Jake to see.

It was another one of the We'll Be Back Soon signs they'd seen on other attractions. But on this one, the hands pointed to three o'clock.

"Do you think maybe…" Furst stopped on a wince. "Nah. Probably not."

But Jake caught on to the other man's line of reasoning and the thought took off like a match set to a line of kerosene. "May I?" He pinched the edge of the laminated card stock between his thumb and forefinger.

"By all means," the other man said, sounding pleased to relinquish the possible evidence along with his suspicions. "Maybe we should see if some of the other locations have these, too?"

Nodding along, Jake pulled his mic from his vest. "See what

time they're showing." He pressed the button to talk. "Hey, Chief?"

Aronson responded right away. "Copy."

"I think Sergeant Furst from Fire may have found something. We're on our way up to see you."

Furst shook his head. "I'm a forensic specialist. I need to sift through some more of this." He nudged a jumble of split two-by-fours and squashed teddy bears with the toe of his boot. "You go ahead. Give it to the colonel with the compliments of the LRFD."

Fifteen minutes later, Aronson stood at one of the tall tables in the arena concourse, looking at a handful of Be Back Soon signs. Some were pristine, like the one set for four o'clock. It had been pinned to the doorjamb at the entrance to the Poultry Barn, not far from the spot where Jake and Max had found the storage container under the table.

Laid out beside the one from the gate, set to twelve, and the sign suction-cupped to the shattered glass door of the Arkansas Building, it looked fresh out of the package.

"Cattle Barn 1 is set to nine o'clock, and the Swine Barn to seven," Jake pointed out.

"I sent a team down to the pirate ride," Aronson told them. "You said you saw one in the cattle barn?"

Jake shrugged. "Pretty sure I did. It was set to six o'clock. I remember thinking the cows would get dinner before me," he explained.

Colonel Aronson stared at him, his expression bland. "I take it your shift usually ends at seven?"

"Yes, sir."

"Colonel Aronson?" The disembodied voice of a young-sounding woman interrupted a murmured debate about measuring time in meals.

The older man picked up his radio and spoke into it. "Go ahead."

"We have the sign from the ride," the woman on the other end informed him. "It's showing two o'clock."

Aronson straightened. "It's as good a goose to chase as any. Go find some more of these cards."

Chapter Nine

Cassidy's mind swam with confusion. Between the blast, the near confrontation with Jake about their past, and hours spent spinning on this never-ending merry-go-round, she was completely undone.

She was so tired of watching him walk away. She was sick—literally sick—of being stuck on this ride. She was also feeling fairly fed up with the teams working the site looking at her like she was some kind of helpless heroine. She was working this case as hard as any of them.

And with a bomb strapped to her back.

Maybe not her brightest idea, but she'd acted on instinct. And she'd do it again. Probably.

The click of toenails on metal dragged her out of her sulk. She turned to find Max standing at the edge of the platform,

"You're right," she said, addressing the dog as if he were holding up his end of the conversation. "I would. I couldn't let an innocent kid walk around with it, could I? What if he'd gotten on the bus? Who knows what this lunatic might do."

Max opened his mouth as if to speak, but then he simply started panting.

"Yeah, yeah," she said, dismissing his nonverbal commentary with a wave of her hand. "Well, sometimes someone actually has to step up and be the hero, you know?"

The dog's eyebrows twitched, then he turned and plopped

his rump down, staring out at the midway, his eyes bright and ears standing at attention.

"Don't be cute."

Max cast her a pitying glance, then smiled his doggie smile and returned to his surveillance. Cassidy decided to take a cue from the dog and get busy finding something else to do.

"Fine. You can't help it."

She picked up the map Jake had left behind and unfolded it on the bench beside her, smoothing the creases. Jake had marked each of the locations where a device had been located, but they were still on the hunt.

Cassidy was afraid the tormentor may have thrown out any plan they'd originally had when she hadn't played by the rules, but there must have been one at the start. They'd taken a gamble in giving the bag to Darien to start but, given the tone of the messages sent, they'd seen it as a calculated risk. They'd assumed—correctly—she would step between the boy and danger.

But why scatter bombs around the fairgrounds to start? Simply intent on causing as much mayhem as possible? Was it a mind game? Most likely both, she decided.

The teams had been lucky so far. Despite the sheer number of explosions, only minor injuries had been sustained. And Cassidy wanted to keep it that way.

The sound of a helicopter approaching made her heart drop into the depths of her belly. She knew any daydreams she might have entertained as far as keeping this confrontation under wraps was shot. The fairgrounds were surrounded by residential neighborhoods. Even at midday during the work week, someone had undoubtedly heard the blasts and called the police. Local law enforcement was already on the scene, of course, but the neighbors didn't know what was happening.

Bud and the rest of her security team had done their best to dodge the questions of the reporters on site at the time of the initial threat, but now… It was only natural for the public to turn to the media for answers. She purposefully avoided thinking about social media. It was beast no one could contain.

Still, she was hopeful. If they could get through this and find out who exactly was responsible, they might be able to get the grounds in good enough condition to open the fair to the public.

But they had to get through it first.

In one piece.

Maybe if she could find the pattern, they could locate the rest of the devices before things got any more out of hand.

Staring down at the map, she let her vision go blurry. Then she blinked it into focus. The second time she did this, she thought maybe she'd spotted a possible pattern.

Without taking her eyes off the map, she grappled for the pen tucked into the crease of the bench. Drawing lightly, so as not to mark up the document too much, she started sketching a loose arc connecting the north gate to the buildings lining the outer perimeter of the fairgrounds proper. When she completed the circle, she was gratified to see it encompassed many of the bomb sites already identified.

She made note of a couple of outbuildings that hadn't been on the list she'd given Jake to start. Then, placing the tip of the pen on the carousel, she drew a smaller circle inside the boundary she'd already created. The line ran straight through the Ferris wheel standing silent sentry next to her, to the duck pond game and through the kiddie rides.

Flexing her jaw, she lifted her head and looked out over the midway. "I see you," she whispered to her unseen terrorist.

Max made a soft, inquisitive noise. It reminded her of old Scooby-Doo cartoons. The canine vocalization of a question mark.

"I think we're getting there, buddy."

The dog turned his head, as if awaiting a command, but did not move from his post.

Cassidy stared down at the map again, willing the key to

this puzzle to come to her. "They're getting closer," she said distractedly. "What's next?"

Beside her, her phone buzzed, skittering along the bench.

She jerked as if struck by a bullet. The cell Bud had brought to her was not the device lighting up. It was her phone. A text notification blared across the screen. Dread pooled in her gut. "Oh no." She reached for the device. "Why can't you leave me alone?"

Max keened softly and moved closer, his amber eyes liquid with concern.

She opened the messaging app and found two terrifying words glaring back at her.

I'm bored

A choked laugh of disbelief escaped her. She pressed a hand to her chest, but it did little to quell the hammering of her heart. "Dude, this is your idea of a good time, not mine."

As if sensing the uptick of tension in her, Max moved to sit directly in front of her, his backside planted firmly on her toes. She gave the dog a puzzled frown. "You trying to hold me captive, too?"

Then something changed.

At first, she couldn't quite put her finger on what it was. A breeze blew her hair back from her cheek. She looked up at the cables and trailers scattered along the back of the midway. Something was different. It was definitely breezier than a minute earlier. Was there weather moving in? Without thinking, she glanced up, but the canopy of the carousel was now her sky. She turned to look out at the concourse and found the sun was still shining brightly.

Max's toenails clattered when he shifted, throwing his weight into her. "Hey now," she chided.

And then it all clicked.

The carousel was moving faster.

Whipping her head around as they sailed past the controls, she expected to find someone standing near them. But the area around the ride was clear. She locked on to the damaged food stand, silently counting the seconds as she zipped by.

She wasn't imagining it.

Max sat with his front paws splayed wide, struggling to hold his ground against the increase in centrifugal force. Cassidy placed a hand atop the shepherd's head, unsure if she was trying to steady him or herself. Either way, it seemed to help them both.

"Someone hit the gas, huh, boy?" Head swiveling, she scanned the entire three-sixty view for anyone who might be responsible for the sudden acceleration.

Then her phone buzzed.

Another message from another number.

Turns out time doesn't fly when you're having fun. Let's speed things up.

"Oh no." A part of her wanted to surrender to what felt like the inevitable outcome. Give up. Give in. Throw in the towel and tell whoever was doing this they'd won.

She was over it. And if they asked for something—anything—in moment, she would concede to their demands if it meant an end to the torment.

But they'd made no demands, only taunts. There could be no negotiation because they'd asked for nothing. Was it truly possible they only wanted to torment her? What had she ever done to deserve this? And how, if she was the target, could she make it all stop? At this point, she'd gladly give herself over to whatever outcome the perpetrator deemed optimal. But this needed to stop. She needed to get off this ride.

As if sensing the conciliatory direction on her thoughts, Max turned his head and placed his large muzzle on her thigh. Cassidy found herself staring into his stern, vigilant expression, and all thought of concession fled.

He wasn't giving up.

No one else wanted to give up. Max, Jake and every other person on site was doing the work. Putting themselves in danger and totally focused on achieving the best possible outcome. They weren't throwing themselves pity parties or telepathically negotiating with terrorists because they were tired and their backs ached.

Sinking her teeth into her bottom lip, she reached for her radio.

"Hey, Jake," she called. Her voice quavered a bit, but there was no point in trying to pretend she was anything other than completely freaked out. There was a ghost in this machine, and she was stuck here with it.

"Copy," came his reply.

"I think y'all need to come down here," she said. "Someone's messing with this thing."

A beat passed before his reply came through. "Messing with what thing?"

"The carousel," she clarified. "Our friend on the other end said they wanted to speed things up. I do believe they meant it literally."

"Come again?"

"Either the motor on this ride is malfunctioning, or our bomber has a way to control the speed." She drew a deep breath. "Regardless, I don't think we're going to have as much time as we'd like to find those other devices."

"You have new messages?"

Cassidy found herself hoping the breathlessness she heard in his response meant he was on his way. As much as she wanted this to be over, she wanted the good guys to be the ones speeding up the timeline.

"I do," she answered. "You might ask Colonel Aronson to come, too. I think this may be a game changer."

Within ten minutes, both men jumped aboard the carousel while another team inspected the ride controls in an attempt to determine why she'd picked up speed. Cassidy heard one tech say something about a throttle and another reply in the negative, but for the most part, she was absorbed by the debate taking place between Jake and his superior.

"Sir, I think we should—"

"I heard you the first five times, Donovan," Aronson interrupted. "But I am in charge of this investigation, and I disagree. I'll ask the other K-9 teams to search for any devices we haven't yet located, but I have to cover investigation on the five that have blown, and we have to disrupt the circuitry on those we've identified."

"But, sir—" Jake tried again.

Aronson shook his head. "You can consult with Ms. Walker on what she thinks the most likely spots are," he said with a nod to Cassidy. "I agree with your perimeter assessment, Ms. Walker. I do believe the circle is tightening. Unfortunately, I also agree with your conclusion we're standing at ground zero."

"I have a feeling this might be one of those rare times when I hate being right," she said dryly.

The older man's face softened slightly. "Is there anything I can do for you, Ms. Walker? Anything you need?"

"Other than a trip to the ladies' room?" It was a sad attempt at levity. "No, sir."

Jake frowned as he looked around. "May we can rig something—"

This time, Cassidy derailed his train of thought. "Seriously?" She glared at Jake, incredulous. "No, thank you."

"But you've been on here for hours and—"

"And I'm good," she insisted. "Sheesh. Go find a bomb or something."

He scowled at her. "We have got to find a way to slow this down."

Cassidy looked around, then shrugged. "Honestly? Moving faster is a little easier to stomach." She gave them a wry smile. "But don't tell my fan club I said so. They go any faster, it might fling me straight off." She paused as if considering the possibility. "On second thought…"

"Ha, ha," Jake scoffed.

She quirked an eyebrow. "I'm not entirely kidding."

"You can't jump now," Jake shot back. "You'd look like one of those jokers who put their foreheads on a baseball bat and spin before trying to run to first base."

Thankfully, Colonel Aronson stepped in to halt their inane conversation before it veered into the ridiculous. "The speed is going to make it harder to gauge the timing on jumping down," he commented, eying the concourse whizzing past warily.

"I guess we should get to it," Jake said, leaning down to check Max's harness. "You'll be okay here?"

Cassidy resisted the urge to roll her eyes. There was still a bomb strapped to her back. How okay did he want her to be?

But he meant well, and good intentions earned him the benefit of minimal snark. She inclined her head. "You go on. I need to call Emma Parker and see if she's come up with anything," she said, reaching for the phone Bud supplied.

"Emma's the best we have when it comes to this sort of thing," Aronson said with a nod of approval. "Let me know if the two of you come up with any leads."

She forced a tight smile. "Will do."

She watched as the two men and the dog moved to the edge of the platform and held on, measuring the pace of the increased velocity.

Jake and Max leaped first, the dog landing with far more grace than his partner. Aronson hesitated a beat too long, then opted to hang on for one more circuit. Not wanting to make him self-conscious, Cassidy made a point of looking away. He made the leap at last, and she lifted her head as soon as she heard his boots hit the asphalt with a slap.

Jake was by the commander's side in an instant, offering a steadying arm. She watched as the two men made their way out of the warren of aluminum gates, their heads bent together in conversation. Max trotted along at Jake's side, ears twitching and a spring in his step, clearly pleased to be back in the game.

Still, he turned to look at her.

And as if moving in synchronization, Jake did, too.

Cassidy lifted a hand in farewell then held up the mobile phone for them to see. She'd saved Special Agent Parker's number when the two of them had spoken earlier in the day. And though she was entirely certain she agreed with the team commander's decision to move forward with efforts to disarm the IEDs, it felt like they were finally making some progress in figuring this game out.

She sat back as much as the pack would allow and watched the world pass by. After a moment, she let her gaze go unfocused and her mind sharpened. There was something in the records. She knew it. The question was, would she be able to locate this particular perpetrator in her past?

Tapping the screen to place the call to the cyber crime specialist, she set her jaw. If whoever was on the other end of this wanted to move faster, so would they.

Emma Parker answered on the first ring. "Hey." Her greeting was distracted. Clearly, she was in the depths of her research. "You were a busy bee in the service."

"Just doing my job, ma'am." Cassidy affected a laconic drawl. "And I'm still a busy bee. When I'm not being held hostage by bomb-building maniacs, that is. Have you found anything interesting?"

"I've isolated some of the more serious cases you worked on. Not finding any suspects with a background in explosives, but of course, these days it hardly matters. It's not like the information isn't out there for all to see."

"It certainly is a popular topic for search engines," she said. "I wonder if all those tech gurus anticipated their creations being used for nefarious purposes."

Emma gave a soft snort. "Aside from their own nefarious purposes?"

"Well, yeah," Cassidy conceded. "Read me some of the names and let me see if anything rings any alarm bells."

"Ableton, Foster, Kozlowski, White…" Emma began. "They served the most time in military detention," she added. "There are also those who got off with being dishonorably discharged as accessories to various crimes—Baker, Harlow, Inonichi, Lam—"

A few of the names rang vague bells in Cassidy's memory. "Give me the gist on Kozlowski, White and Baker."

"Looks like Kozlowski was multiple counts of Conduct Unbecoming of an Officer," Emma revealed.

The moment the word "unbecoming" was out of her mouth, Cassidy recalled the details of Kozlowski's case. "Ah, yes, Kozlowski. He was a training officer who liked to get a little too hands-on with his trainees," she said with a scowl.

"Were you one?" Emma asked.

Cassidy shook her head with vehemence even though she knew the other woman could not see her. "No. I wasn't involved in any way other than assisting with the arrest."

"How about White? Looks like he was busted for discharging a firearm during a domestic disturbance," Emma disclosed.

"Yeah, that was a mess."

Cassidy recalled the scene. "Airman White was showing his girlfriend around on base when it became apparent she'd dated another airman in residence prior to meeting Mr. White. The two men exchanged words. We thought the situation was resolved, but Mr. White decided to retrieve an unauthorized weapon from his vehicle and threatened the other airman—"

"Tzarnik," Emma interjected.

"Yes. He pointed the gun at Airman Tzarnik, but when his girlfriend screamed at him, he shifted his aim just enough to put a bullet in the side of a dumpster. Of course, with shots fired, the base went on lockdown. Another security officer was positioned behind the gunman and managed to tackle Airman White before he could get another shot off."

"Any reason for White to come after you in particular?"

"I testified at the Court-Martial," Cassidy said. "But I wasn't the only one."

"Brings us to Baker," Emma prompted. "Trevor Baker, Airman First Class, 19th Maintenance Squadron."

"And he was discharged?" Cassidy paused to search her memory.

"Yes. Dishonorable Discharge. Accessory Possession and Absent Without Leave." Emma read the charges off, noting, "He was a munitions guy."

"Oh!" She sat up straighter. "Yeah, I remember Baker. He and his brother—" She broke off at the sound of another explosion coming from the south end of the fairgrounds.

The chopper lazily circling the grounds swooped back into view. Cassidy grimaced when she spotted the logo for a local news affiliate on the tail of the craft.

"I have to go." She ended the call as she stood. The butterflies in her stomach told her the carousel wasn't the only thing about to start moving too fast.

Chapter Ten

Walking away from Cass was getting harder each time he had to do it. It had been all he could do to listen to the instructions Aronson was firing off as they trudged back up the hill. They'd paused to watch the team covering the post-explosion investigation at Cattle Barn 4 before heading to the arena to catch up with the other team leads. He was running through a list of possible locations to check, bearing in mind the perimeters Cass had drawn.

"What's the relationship between you and Cassidy Walker?" The colonel's blunt question startled Jake from his thoughts.

Alarm bells rang in his head as he glanced at the older man. But Aronson only gave him profile. The man's jaw was relaxed and his expression as neutral as his tone.

Jake wasn't buying it for a moment.

He stalled for time. If the site commander was asking, he obviously considered his acquaintance with the main character in this farce to be relevant. And if he wanted to remain active on this case, he needed pick his way through this minefield carefully. Wetting his lips, he opted to go with the barest facts.

"We were high school classmates, but we haven't been in contact for years."

"Years?" Aronson slid him a sidelong glance.

"Not since college."

"You seem to know one another fairly well," the other man said, allowing his skepticism to creep into his tone.

"We did at one time, but as I said, it's been years," Jake repeated, refusing to give up anything more than the most basic facts.

"But you're worried about her," he persisted.

Puzzled by the comment, Jake frowned. "Of course, I am. She walked right into a trap set by some jerk who likes to blow things up."

"A trap we believe was set for her," Aronson pointed out.

Jake slowed as they approached the tinted-glass doors of Barton Coliseum. "What exactly is your concern, sir?"

Aronson halted altogether, his hand on the door handle. "I'm concerned by your insistence on running down there every chance you get to sit next to a woman who may or may not have a bomb on her back. I know we run toward danger, son, but you may be taking it too far." He took a deep breath. "My concern is you may not be approaching your work objectively. Or conducting your searches thoroughly—"

"Respectfully, sir, I was the one who ID'd the location of multiple devices—"

"With Ms. Walker's help," he interjected.

"Who better to help?" Jake struggled to keep his rising impatience in check. "If the head of fairgrounds security was standing safe and secure in this arena, I'd be consulting with her here. But she isn't. And yes, we know each other…*knew* each other…when we were kids. And yes, she is wearing what we have identified to be an explosive device, but we're taking all the necessary precautions—"

"You think sitting next to her at the top of each hour is taking precautions?" The commander scoffed. "You think leaving your partner with her when you aren't there is the cautious thing to do?" he demanded, gesturing to Max. "How many thousands of dollars did it cost to train him, Donovan? You're treating a skilled detection dog like an emotional support animal."

Jake's hand instinctively went to Max's smooth head. "I beg to differ…sir."

Colonel Aronson blew out a tired breath. "Listen, son, I know it can be difficult when there's an…acquaintance involved in a case. If I need to call in one of the other K-9 units—"

"No, sir," Jake interrupted before the other man could give voice to the notion of replacing him. "I promise you, Max and I are on it."

The site commander studied him for a long, silent moment, then gave a brisk nod. "I'm getting fed up with dancing to this joker's tune."

"We all are, sir," Jake assured him.

"Let's get cracking then," Aronson said, yanking the door open wide.

Jake followed him into the dim interior of the arena. A few team leads were hovering around one of the tall counters encircling a support post. Jake was happy to join them there while Aronson conferred with Bud Thompson and a woman dressed in a bright blue pantsuit.

He leaned closer to Evan Furst. "Who's the suit?"

"Governor's press secretary." The other man kept a wary eye on the suit. "Things are about to get interesting."

"Like they haven't been already?"

Colonel Aronson broke away from the small knot of people and came over to them. "We're splitting up on detection. LRPD will cover the outer perimeter, including the auxiliary buildings," he announced.

Jake murmured to Furst, "I hope they strike out in those buildings. We moved about a dozen head of expensive cattle there earlier in the day."

Aronson turned to him. "I'm putting you on the inner circle. I need you to cover most of the arcade games. We've hardly looked at any of them except the remains of the duck game."

Jake nodded, wondering if the colonel had given him the

inner circle because it would keep him close to Cass, or if he'd given up on trying to make him stay away. Either way, he wasn't about to argue with the man. He stood, shifting his weight impatiently as the other teams were assigned to investigation or intervention. The moment they were dismissed, he pivoted for the door.

They were stepping out into the afternoon sunlight when an explosion sent them diving for ground.

Max and the LRPD detection dog, a black Labrador named Holmes, strained against their leads, unbothered by the noise but keen in their desire to track down the source of the sulfurous scent wafting toward them.

The glass doors flew open behind them. Aronson and the other officers assembled spilled out onto the asphalt apron.

"Where?" Aronson demanded, head swiveling as Jake and the LRPD handler dusted themselves off.

"South." Jake nodded in the direction of a thin plume of smoke rising above the buildings behind the arena. "Looks like Poultry."

Colonel Aronson snatched his radio from its clip. "Yardley, come in," he barked.

Static crackled, then a voice came across loud and clear. "Yardley, sir."

"What's happening?" the commander demanded.

"Sir, we have a failed intervention."

"Details," Aronson prompted.

"No casualties. Minimal property damage. Well, aside from Rex," he amended.

Jake winced as Aronson let loose with an expletive on behalf of them all. The Arkansas State Police had introduced their robotic dog the previous year to great fanfare. The four-legged android controlled by a bomb squad specialist was often sent to assess the IED a team had identified and to determine the best path to intervention in disarming the device.

"Damage assessment?"

"Looks like we're going to be back to using old Rufus for a while," the man reported, referring to the less-sophisticated robot the LRPD used. "I don't think any of the birds were harmed. This was not very powerful. Noisy, for sure, and Rex was right up in it, but other than disabling the bot, it didn't do much damage."

"I'm sending a team in to help with investigation."

Aronson's eyes skipped over Jake. "You and you," he said, pointing to a couple of firefighters. "Go check the site." Turning back to Jake and the detection team from LRPD, he said, "I'm getting tired of this bozo setting off firecrackers for fun. Find me the last three and let's get them disarmed."

"Last two." Jake wanted to bite back the correction, but it was out there, so instead he bit the tip of his tongue.

"Excuse me?" Aronson's brows lowered like thunderclouds.

"It's two, sir. We've located nine on the grounds, but we know where the tenth one is." The colonel stared back at him, his expression blank. "It's strapped to Cassidy Walker's back."

The blunt reminder killed the conversations taking place around them. The site commander's jaw flexed, but he nodded once in acknowledgment. "Right." Aronson turned to the other detection team. "We have two to locate. Go find them."

"Yes, sir."

Aronson's phone lit up. Jake saw the words "Governor's Office" appear on the screen. The head honcho let loose with another soft-spoken expletive before tapping to accept the call.

"Yes, Governor," he said, turning on his heel and marching back into the dim confines of the arena.

Jake noticed none of the other team leads followed the site commander inside. He caught Evan Furst's eye and the shorter man shrugged. "Safer out here with the bombs."

"I hear you." With a smirk and smart salute, Jake clicked his tongue, and he and Max set off down the hill.

But rather than make a beeline for Cass and the carousel, Jake steered the dog to the long line of carnival games along the east side of the concourse. He moved slowly, giving Max enough lead to work his way methodically from one stall to the next while he did a visual inspection.

The bleat of a police warning siren told him they'd likely gathered an audience. The relentless *whop-whop-whop* of a helicopter's rotor added to the already oppressive sense of foreboding. As they moved from a water pistol game to darts, he chanced a glance up at the chopper. Residents of larger cities might be used to the sound of traffic helicopters and the like, but in Little Rock, they usually only saw med flights transporting patients to one of the major hospitals or the occasional military squadron using the Air Force Base for a layover.

The temptation to pull out his phone and check the local news to see what was being said was strong, but he resisted. When Max lingered at the basketball free-throw game, Jake moved in for a closer look. Opening the plywood board that served as a gate, he and his partner stepped into the open space between the counter and the hoops. Jake slanted his head back to check out the enormous stuffed animals and cartoon characters suspended from the netting above the booth.

Turning in the slow circle, he stared up at the three hoops with their chipping plywood backboards. Judging from his days of playing pickup games at the rec center, Jake estimated the goals hung at least a foot higher than regulation would stipulate. No doubt the rims were a good inch smaller in diameter, too, he thought with a smirk.

A high-pitched whine of impatience drew his attention. He turned to find Max sitting directly in front of the counter where the barker would stand taunting people into taking a shot.

"What did you find, boy?"

Max gave a single bark and Jake's eyebrows shot up. Whatever his partner had located was not explosive. Most likely herbal, Jake mused as he moseyed up to the counter. He certainly couldn't fault Trooper Max for his diligence.

"Something stinky, huh?" He rummaged around on the shelf below the counter. His hand fell on a soft bundle of fabric. He pulled out a felt bag with the logo of an expensive brand of liquor embroidered on it. Max gave it another sniff and confirmed his suspicions with another single bark.

Jake smiled as he pulled open the drawstring bag and took a whiff himself. "Whew-wee," he said, waving a hand in front of his face to disperse the skunklike odor. "Way to go, man," he said with a chuckle, then gave the dog a congratulatory pat on the head.

But Max wasn't letting him off easy. The stubborn cuss stayed put until Jake relented and reached into his pocket for a dog treat.

"You're turning out to be quite the extortionist," he commented as Max gobbled up the morsel.

Without any sign of remorse, the dog trotted toward the entrance to the booth, satisfied with his work.

Jake looked down at the bag in his hand, then tucked it back onto the shelf. He'd let one of the guys from the LRPD know where they'd found it. Hopefully, they'd be able to nab the owner with it in their possession.

"Hold up, buddy." Jake stood his ground when Max reached the end of his tether, and the dog sat to wait for him to catch up.

The lingering scent of cooking oil and fried onions coming down the hill from the food court made his stomach grumble. He couldn't remember if he'd taken more than two bites of the sandwich Cass shared with him.

They started out again but slowed as they approached the site where the duck pond game once stood. Max practically pressed his nose into the asphalt as Jake gave him a minute to explore the scents. He pressed his lips together when he caught sight of Cass sailing past them.

She sat facing forward on the bench, a phone pressed to her ear. How she'd managed to survive all these hours without emptying her stomach, he'd never know. But that was Cass.

Tough.

Stubborn.

Determined.

Amazing.

He watched as she swiped at her hair, catching as much as she could in one hand and holding it back from her face. He smiled when she dropped it almost immediately, needing to gesticulate as she spoke.

He stood rooted to the spot, letting Max sniff to his heart's content while he drank in the sight of her. The neat blazer she wore was now rumpled and no doubt stained from her attempts to stay fed and hydrated. Though her golden-brown hair flew loose around her face, he remembered the way she'd struggled to pull a comb through it after riding with the car window rolled down. Jake had no doubt it would be a tangle of snarls when she got off the ride.

And they would get her off there.

He backed up a step, preparing to lead Max to the next stall in line, but a second before he turned away, Cass came around again, and this time, she raised a hand in a wave.

Jake waved back, then pointed to Max and the ring-toss game farther down the line. Cass tipped her chin up in acknowledgment, then she disappeared again.

"Come on, Max, let's try to get down this row before they make us back off." Time was ticking away, and their tormentor was getting impatient. They didn't have minute to waste.

They'd barely stepped through the barrier leading to the rear of the booth when a buzzing noise snagged his attention. He searched the sky, but Max turned around, his superior hearing homing in on the source much faster.

A drone.

Black and spiderlike, it flew low along the asphalt walkway. Jake narrowed his eyes, watching as the module mounted on the top pivoted in a slow sweep. He took an involuntary step forward as the buzzing grew louder. From his vantage point, Jake couldn't tell if its purpose was surveillance or conveyance. Drones were used to deliver all sorts of mayhem these days. As it approached, he decided this one would not have a chance.

He watched as it made its way down the row. It banked slightly and sunlight glinted off glass. A camera, not a bomb.

Relief pulsed through him, but it was quickly chased by annoyance.

He couldn't see any marking on the plastic casing, nor had there been any discussion of law enforcement deploying any as part of the investigation. Narrowing his eyes, he inspected it as closely as he could from a distance. It looked exactly like a model he'd seen stacked high at the warehouse club where he stocked up on paper and canned goods.

His first impulse was to reach for his service weapon but shooting it out of the sky was not the best answer. The machine presented no identifiable threat to human life. He could shoot it down and mount a decent defense given all that had happened, but the moment he discharged his weapon, a veritable mountain of paperwork and meetings would drop onto his head like a cartoon anvil.

Besides, the toy might belong to their bomber. If he could knock it down without destroying it, they may be able to lift a fingerprint or some other useful information off it.

He looked around, and sure enough, he spotted a better alternative.

A wooden pole stretching about six feet long and sporting a metal hook drilled into the end leaned up against the corner of the booth. Jake recalled seeing carnival workers using similar tools to pull down the larger prizes they dangled high above the contestants' heads.

"Stay," he ordered Max. Then, dropping his end of the dog's lead, he took hold of the pole with both hands.

The drone approached from his left, so Jake slipped out and around a neighboring booth in hopes of sneaking up on it before its operator became aware.

It was a good plan.

He stepped into the drone's path when it was mere feet away and took a wild swipe at it. He clipped one of the offset rotors and caused it to wobble, but the device was far from disabled.

The drone spun around, then the whirring intensified and it began to rise. Jake knew he had one more shot at it before it flew completely out of reach. Gripping the end of the pole like a Louisville Slugger, Jake planted his feet like they'd taught him in junior deputy baseball and swung clean and smooth.

The pole connected with a cringe-inducing *thwack*. Bits of shattered plastic rained down around him. The body of the drone clattered to the ground about ten feet in front of him.

Dragging his new weapon, Jake approached with caution. The soles of his boots crunched on a bit of plastic and he danced to the side, rising onto his toes in an effort not to trample any possible evidence. He stopped about five feet from the site of the crash, planted the end of the pole on the pavement, and turned it over so the hook extended toward the downed device.

He flipped the casing over and spotted the camera lens. After few more pokes with the hook, he whistled sharply and Max came trotting out to join him, his lead trailing on the ground.

"What have we got?"

Max lowered his head, his forehead creasing in concentration as he began to sniff the area, moving in the methodical grid he was taught as a puppy. After a couple of minutes, the dog shook off any suspicion of explosives, then wandered back to Jake's side.

Satisfied, Jake gave the dog a pat and a treat. "Good boy. We like it when there are no bombs."

Unzipping a pocket on Max's vest, he pulled out an evidence bag and a pair of latex gloves. The dog danced to the side, annoyed to have his equipment ransacked. Jake chuckled but persisted. "You're the best packhorse a guy could ever have."

Snapping on the gloves, he began picking up every piece of matte-black plastic he could locate on the blacktop. He was still stooping and scraping when Max let out a woof of impatience, his face turned in the direction of the carousel.

"Yeah, well, why don't you grow yourself some thumbs? It would go faster of you could help," he chided his partner.

For his part, Jake was doing his level best to not check the carousel. Colonel Aronson's questions and the implication he could be removed from the case rang in his ears. If he was going to stick around until the end of this mess, he needed to play it cooler than he had been.

"Much cooler," he mumbled, bending to pick up the drone carcass.

A tiny red light blinked slowly on the top. It was a minuscule distress signal. But it would go unanswered. Using the tip of his gloved finger, he pressed and held the power button until the light blinked out. With a groan, he straightened and walked over to where Max sat impatiently waiting.

"We need to run this up to the boss," Jake said, shifting the drone and evidence bag of parts into one hand. He let loose with another grunt as he swooped down to take up the dog's lead. His muscles were sore from walking the fairgrounds. The tension of the situation didn't help. Nor did laying eyes on Cass for the first time in years.

Jake rolled up to his full height and tilted his chin to the sky, giving every aching muscle a big stretch as he focused on breathing deep. No matter how hard he stretched, a part of him was still doubled over from the gut punch of recognition when her eyes had first met his.

Recognition and wariness.

As if he posed as much of a threat to her as the bomber targeting her.

This time, Max had to quick-step to keep pace with him. As they wove past the wreckage of the duck pond stall, Jake kept his jaw clenched tight. He didn't dare glance in the direction of the carousel. If he did, he'd get caught up in her gravitational pull.

And he couldn't go there. Not when he could see Colonel Aronson charging down the hill, headed in their direction. He'd almost made it past the mangled corn dog stand when he heard her call out.

"Jake?"

He kept walking.

"Jake, I need to talk to you," she shouted.

He gave his head a sharp shake but stayed the course.

"Jacob Michael Donovan!"

She escalated to the use of his full name at the exact same time Aronson bellowed, "Donovan!"

Their voices melded in a strange sort of angry harmony on the three syllables of his last name. It drew him up short. Glancing from Aronson's stormy expression to Cass's high-colored outrage, he shook his head in bewilderment.

He held up the broken surveillance equipment as if the fruit of his prowess might be enough to ward them off any reprimand. "Someone was flying a drone over the scene. I think it may be long to our guy."

But even as the words left his lips, the triumph he'd felt in downing the drone shriveled into a tight ball and lodged in his throat. For some reason, neither of them was celebrating.

Jake got the feeling he'd done something very, very wrong.

Chapter Eleven

Cassidy stood at the edge of the platform, one hand wrapped around a pole, the other resting on the seahorse's head. She pressed the phone to her ear, but she couldn't concentrate on what the woman on the other end of the call was saying. Not when Jake was stuck between her and a hard-faced superior.

She ended the call she'd been on without another word. She wouldn't have to worry about getting a call back. Within minutes, every news outlet in the region would be blowing up her phone. She smiled, thankful for the new phone she was using.

Craning her neck to look back, she caught Jake looking down at the hunk of smashed electronics in his hand as if he wasn't exactly certain how it came to be in his possession.

"What the— What were you thinking?" Colonel Aronson shouted as he closed the distance to Jake.

Cassidy ached to leap from the carousel and run up to join them.

"Sir, I—"

But Jake didn't get a chance to utter another word of explanation. The colonel thrust a cell phone into Jake's face. Cassidy's own cheeks burned as he took a step back. He tilted his head as if trying to get the screen to come into focus, but she knew exactly what he was watching.

Because Emma Parker had forwarded the same video sent to her phone mere minutes before.

Sinking back down onto the bench, she caught snippets of the man's shouts as he dressed Jake down for endangering himself and everyone around him by acting so impulsively.

Every so often, Jake would attempt to interject and explain, but it was clear the commander was having none of it. Words like "payload" and "clearance" and "renegade" were sprinkled with some mild expletives and served cold. Though she'd planned to give him a piece of her mind for acting in such a reckless, impulsive way, she didn't like hearing him take it from someone else.

Drawing a deep breath, she focused on the toes of her shoes as she waited for the colonel to wind down. Oddly enough, the increased speed of the ride helped with the nausea she'd suffered earlier. She eyed the balled-up wrapper containing the remnants of the sandwich she and Jake had attempted to share, and wondered if she could get the fire department trainee to bring her another.

Colonel Aronson's decibel level dropped significantly by the time she made her next trip around to the concourse. Now the two men stood examining the remains of the drone and what appeared to be a collection of parts contained in a plastic evidence bag. The next time she saw them, she noticed Jake was still wearing bright blue latex gloves.

She knew in an instant what had caused the calm, cool, collected man she'd encountered earlier in the day to grab a long wooden pole and go Luke Skywalker on the drone. He'd believed he was bringing down the camera their perpetrator was using to watch them. Watch *her*.

And if his assumption had been correct, she may have had the chance to ditch the backpack and jump off this wild ride.

But he'd been wrong.

The drone was piloted by a seventeen-year-old boy named Bryce, who lived a few blocks away from the fairgrounds and wanted to get a better look at whatever was causing the commotion. When he'd seen the wreckage left by some of the explosions, Bryce did what any seventeen-year-old in possession of some cool footage would do—he live-streamed the drone's flight.

The local news affiliates had picked up the stream and were showing it live on the air.

That meant a good portion of the Central Arkansas viewing audience got to see a State Trooper in full tactical gear taking a grand-slam-worthy swing at a teenager's toy.

Biting her lip, Cassidy pressed Play on the video again. There was Jake, looking handsome and dead serious, swinging a ridiculous pole like he was going after a piñata.

Though she had to admit his final swing showed much better form. It was high, for sure, but the follow-through was major-league. She paused the video at the spot where his strong arms coiled around to his shoulder and his long legs twisted around each other.

Gorgeous form.

Pressing her mouth into a flat line, she calculated the short time it would take for Jake Donovan to transform from hapless cop flailing at a drone to internet hunk intent on saving the day. A wry smile tugged at the corner of her lips as she envisioned his baffled reaction to viral attention. But it disappeared the moment she saw Jake turn in her direction. His brow was lowered, his expression thunderous. He wasn't the sort of man who'd readily take criticism for doing what he thought was right.

This flash of stubborn insubordination appealed to her more than she wanted to admit.

Her personal phone rang and she winced. Glancing down, she saw she had a number of messages from unknown callers piled up in her voicemail and text app. Heaven knew how many more calls she'd miss. These days, with witnesses eager to play reporter and wielding their own camera crews, it was impossible to outpace the press.

She was thankful for the privacy setting that sent unknown

callers to voicemail. Her new phone rang and she saw Emma Parker's name flash on the screen.

"Walker here," she said, her gaze straying to the two men caught up in heated conversation.

"You get my message?" Emma asked without preamble.

"I did. Jake's getting chewed out as we speak."

"Poor guy. I'd have done the same thing," the special agent said.

"Any luck with the files?" Cassidy asked, purposefully turning away from Jake's dressing-down.

"I think Baker is our guy," Cassidy said.

The hum on the other end told her Emma had been thinking along the same lines, but might not be entirely convinced. "Based on? All we have is a lot of conjecture and a strong hunch."

Cassidy laughed. "Oh, well, it's a lot then. Book him."

"Ha. If I could be a jury of one, I would. I am on my way over to his house to feel him out, though."

Cassidy's brows shot up. "He still lives here?"

She didn't bother to mask the surprise in her tone. Most people assigned to the base were transplants. Military personnel who went wherever they were assigned. They were deployed when necessary, but unless they had some tie to Arkansas outside of their time in the service, they usually moved on.

"Is he an Arkansan?"

"He was born in California, but it looks like the family moved to Texarkana when he was young."

"I wonder why he stayed after being discharged."

"Married a woman from Jacksonville not long after he got out. Everything I find points to a residence in Southwest Little Rock."

"And you're heading over there yourself? What are you going to do, ring the doorbell and ask him if he's been setting off bombs at the fairgrounds?"

"Heck of an icebreaker," Emma said with a chuckle. "No, I found out he applied to join the Little Rock Fire Department a couple times. Looks like he didn't make the cut. But that doesn't mean I can't follow up as part of a, uh, background check."

"Do the State Police perform background checks for municipalities?" Cassidy's brows drew down into a frown.

"No, but I doubt Baker knows how the process goes. I flash my badge, tell him I saw where he's applied to the LRFD, and I want to talk to him about his discharge—both true—and see if I can get a read on him." Cassidy caught a long gust of an exhale. "He worked in munitions, remember?"

"Right." Something itched at the back of her mind. Something Cassidy had wanted to tell Emma when they'd discussed Baker before, but she couldn't recall what it was.

"Okay. I'll check back with you after and give you the rundown."

"Sounds good."

She looked up in time to see Jake step back, thrusting the bag and the disabled drone at Aronson, a mutinous set to his jaw. The beeps indicating the end of the call sounded in her ear as the angry colonel turned on his heel and marched back up the hill.

Cassidy couldn't take her eyes off Jake. His back was ramrod-straight and his chin angled up in defiance, but still he looked…lost. Cassidy scooted to the edge of the bench, but she lost her line of vision. But by the time she came out the other side, he was heading straight for her.

When he stepped around the gate, she graced him with her widest smile. "Way to go, slugger."

He shot her a glare. "Don't you start, too."

"Your boss didn't look happy with you," she commented as he and Max jumped onto the ride.

Jake grabbed the nearest pole, planting his feet wide and keeping his knees bent until he grew accustomed to the ride's velocity. "He's not exactly my boss, but no, he's not happy with me."

She gave Max a welcome pat, then peered up at the man looming over her. "My phone has been blowing up. Good thing I'm not answering it."

He grimaced. "Sorry."

She gestured to the bench across from her. "Sit. I can't keep looking up."

He dropped onto the seat. "Nauseous?"

"Crick in my neck." She rolled her shoulders and the nylon straps of the backpack chafed against her bare skin. "Our cub reporter was streaming on YouTube and chatting live with one of the local anchors when you made your debut."

"I hear it was a teenager."

"A kid named Bryce," she said with a nod. "You're going to owe him a new drone."

"He shouldn't have been flying it over an active crime scene," Jake responded through clenched teeth.

"Agreed, but this is the world we live in these days." Then she grinned at him again. "The footage is awesome. I bet there are at least a dozen memes already."

He quirked a single brow. "I was aiming for GIF status."

"The way you took aim at the drone? I have no doubt you'll be swinging through the interwebs like a guy bitten by a radioactive spider by the end of the night."

"I always liked Superman better."

"I know. You like the real-deal heroes, not the guys who have a bone to pick with the world."

"I'm not hero enough to willingly strap a bomb onto my back," he shot back.

"Nah, only antiheroes do things like run down a dock with a big smoking bomb."

"Like in the old Batman TV show?" He closed his eyes in a long blink, and when he reopened them, she'd swear the light in those blue depths burned a little brighter. Either that, or she was hallucinating.

"Uh-huh."

Jake leaned in, clasping his hands between his knees as he studied her intently. "How are things going?"

"Other than the dozens of media calls I'll have to field because you decided to play home run derby with a drone?"

His lips thinned into a line, but he nodded an acknowledgment. "Yes, other than those."

"I'm peachy," she said, keeping her tone light.

"Do you need some medicine for the nausea?"

She waved the suggestion away. "Actually, the increase in speed is working out better for me." Her phone buzzed in her hand, but she ignored it. "I'm glad I didn't ask Bud to forward the incoming calls from the office to this phone." She gave her head a rueful shake. "I don't have the stamina to do much at the moment."

"Actually, you're doing a lot," he countered.

"As much as anyone parked on a seahorse bench can do," she agreed, her tone dry as desert sand. "Emma Parker is following up on a lead on our suspect."

He nodded. "Colonel Aronson said she was going to question someone you arrested."

Cassidy leaned in, too, bracing her elbows on her knees to help alleviate some of the weight on her back and shoulders. "I barely remember the guy, and his discharge was more than ten years ago. Something doesn't feel right. Why wait so long?"

"Revenge is best served cold?" He hazarded a guess.

She wove her fingers together and squeezed before shaking them out again. "Seems like a stretch. I've been racking my brain, trying to remember everything I can about the incident. Baker's brother was driving him back to the base. We stopped them at the gate because we suspected the brother was driving impaired."

"Was he?"

"Reeked of alcohol, but refused to submit to a field sobriety test."

"Breathalyzer?"

She shook her head. "I tried to get him to do one, but he refused. Claimed since they were still in line to get past the gate, they were technically on city property, not on base and I had no authority."

Jake's eyebrows jumped. "What did you do?"

"Notified Jacksonville police and detained him until they arrived," she said with a shrug.

"Did you arrest the brother?"

"Oh, yeah," she said, nodding emphatically. "Trevor got out of the car, shooting his mouth off about how his brother was going to get him busted, and carrying on. We walked him through to the gatehouse then patted him down. Found enough to charge him with possession with intent to sell."

"And his brother?"

"He was quiet at first," she said, thinking back. She tried to conjure an image of either man, but figured she was likely superimposing the file photo Emma had sent over on whatever scraps of memory she had. "He was too quiet. Barely said a word."

"Jacksonville PD took him in?"

"Yeah. Yeah, he had…so much." She gave a short, sharp laugh. "Driving under the influence, though, would later get thrown out. His lawyer argued we hadn't actually seen the vehicle move, so we couldn't say for certain he was operating it." She gave an indelicate snort, and he shook his head, no doubt pondering the many vagaries of due process, as cops so often do.

"Anyway, he had enough of a stash to stock a small pharmacy. Felony possession with intent to distribute. Also found a handgun." She twisted her lips into a smirky smile. "Unregistered, of course. The elder Mr. Baker had a previous felony conviction."

"Of course he did."

Cassidy ignored his sarcasm, lost to her memories as the events of the long-ago confrontation came rushing back to her.

The rainbow of pills.

An avalanche of plasticine packets.

The skunk stench of weed seeping from the upholstery.

Airman Baker's litany of curses.

His brother's stony silence.

When she lifted her head, she found Jake watching her closely. She could not escape the niggling sensation that she was forgetting something important or the way Jake's stare made her feel squirmy inside. Her stomach rumbled and she latched on to the distraction.

"Hey, I wonder if I can get another sandwich or something? The first one got trampled and, oddly enough, I feel like I could eat now."

The request startled a laugh out of him. "Yeah, I bet you can get your probie friend to bring you something. How's your water?"

She shrugged. "Gone. I think it rolled off." Cassidy turned one direction, then the other, trying to catch sight of the firefighter usually hovering nearby. "Hey, T.B.?" she croaked when she spotted him propped up against one of the generator trailers at the back of the ride.

"Ma'am?" he replied.

But Jake spoke up for her. "Can we get some more water and something to eat brought to Ms. Walker? Nothing with onions though." He paused, turning to look at her, brows knit tightly together. "Or do you eat onions now?"

Her heart slammed into her rib cage and she must have sucked in a breath when she heard him add the special request. She swallowed hard, touched he remembered such tiny details. She shook her head, but her voice was barely more than a whisper. "No. No onions, please."

"Anything else?" T.B. asked, looking past Jake to her.

She forced a weak smile. It went against the grain to ask anyone to go out of their way for her. Especially when they all had much more important things to do. But she had been spinning around on this thing for hours, and her cheeks and lips were parched and windburned.

"Some lip balm? Or petroleum jelly?" The tentative quaver in her voice annoyed her almost as much as asking for help did, but this was where she was at the moment. Hungry and parched in almost every conceivable way.

She glanced down at the phone clutched in her hand as Jake relayed her additional requests. He cast a sidelong glance at her, then added, "And something sweet. A cookie or brownie. Something with some sugar."

She pinned him with a curious stare as he settled back onto the bench. "You think I need sugar?"

He shrugged. "I figured it couldn't hurt."

Cassidy chuckled, her cheeks warming with pleasure despite her best efforts to play it cool with him. "You're probably right."

He tilted his head as he studied her, looking every bit as curious as Max. "You're not saying something."

She shook her head. "I'm not…I can't…" She gave a full-body shake and let out a grunt of frustration, then thumped her temple with two fingers. "There's something right there about the Baker case, but I can't quite pin it down."

"Let's talk about something else for a while. Maybe it will come to you if you're not pressing so hard," he suggested.

Knowing he was right, she waggled the phone at him. "Did Colonel Aronson show you the footage?"

Jake wet his lips, then shook his head. "No. He was too busy telling me what a damn fool I was, and that I might as well have knocked down a hornets' nest."

Leaning in, Cassidy pulled up the message containing the clip and let it play. "I wasn't kidding about your farm. You can still swing for the fences."

Jake's grim expression softened, but his eyes narrowed as he watched. "I don't regret taking it out," he said as the video stopped.

"I would have done the same."

"Aronson tells me the governor's press person is having a fit."

"No doubt."

With Max resting at their feet, they lapsed into companionable conversation, discussing the bureaucracy surrounding their jobs, the members of the various response units they'd encountered throughout the day and the repairs that would need to be addressed if the fair was indeed going to open after all. She had no idea how much time had passed, but it was significant enough that Jake sat up and looked around.

"Your pal must have had to go off site to get some food."

"I guess so." Cassidy scanned the area with each pass. It seemed hard to believe, given how the scent of tantalizing fair food lingered in the air. "Maybe I should have had Manny stay behind after all," she said, tipping her head in the direction of the battered food stand. "I could go for a corn dog."

"I can radio for someone else," he offered.

She waved the offer away. "I'll get Bud to raid my office. I have everything there." She placed a quick call to her second-in-command, who responded right away.

Minutes later, Bud pulled up on his golf cart with bottled water. "I'll go raid your desk drawer for protein bars," he said as he tossed bottle after bottle to Jake, who snagged them like fly balls.

"Hey, in the center drawer there's lip balm and a little bottle of ibuprofen," she called as he climbed into the driver's seat again. Bud raised a hand in acknowledgment then took off.

The mention of the painkillers brought forth the memory of

the stash Trevor Baker's brother had been transporting when the Jacksonville police had searched his car. There was some connection to the brother's arrest she couldn't quite pin down. Cassidy grabbed her phone and jabbed the screen until Agent Parker's number rang through.

Emma answered the call with a harried, "Hello?"

"Have you left Baker's place?"

"A minute ago. Hang on." Emma huffed and puffed, clearly juggling her phone before she came back on the line. "Hey. Sorry. Getting back to my car."

Cassidy held her breath as she waited to hear Agent Parker's findings. "You're still at Baker's place?"

"Parked out front. I don't think this is the Baker we're—"

Emma's assessment was swallowed up by the sound of shattering glass. Cass looked up, taking in Jake's concerned frown.

"Emma, are you okay?"

A string of highly indelicate swear words streamed from the speaker. They were somewhat reassuring but were soon overridden by the sound of squealing tires.

"Parker, what's happening?" Jake demanded.

"Someone threw a brick through my rear window." She swore under her breath, but the words were nearly swallowed up by the roar of her car engine.

"A brick?" Cassidy said, dumbfounded.

But Jake snatched the phone from her fingers and raised it to his lips. "Pull over."

"Uh, negative," Emma responded.

"Are you sure it was a brick?" he demanded, his tone rising with urgency.

The squeal of brakes made both Cassidy and Jake wince. But Emma Parker had moved past swear words. Cassidy stared at Jake, her breath tangled in her throat, her mouth dry, as they listened as a series of clicks and snicks accompanied ragged, shallow breathing.

"Emma?" she shouted into the phone. "Emma, are you okay?"

But Emma didn't answer. There was a grunt and the sound of a car door opening. Cassidy and Jake sat knee to knee, not daring to breathe. He held the phone between them, the green speaker icon lit against a black screen.

Then they heard a sound they'd grown all too accustomed to hearing.

An ear-splitting bang.

Booming reverb.

Screeching metal.

A shower of falling debris.

Then a truly terrifying *whoosh*.

The call dropped and the screen went blank.

Chapter Twelve

Her fault.

This was all because of her.

A thousand thoughts, both useful and inane, swirled through her head in the eerily quiet moments after the call dropped, but one circled back time and time again.

This was all her fault.

Cassidy blinked at Jake. The darkened phone still balanced on his open palm, her disbelief reflected in his eyes. Then his jaw tightened and he tossed the phone into her lap. He grappled with his radio, yanking the clip with a force that made her flinch.

"Command?" he barked into the radio. "Command, come in."

The urgency in the request sent a ripple down her spine. Her toes tingled and her fingers twitched as she came back to her senses. Someone had tried to blow up Special Agent Emma Parker. Someone had blown up Agent Parker's car. With her in it?

Jake's phone rang and he reached for it. "It's Aronson."

"Oh no." The words slipped out on a moan. Colonel Aronson would not be calling Jake unless there was news he didn't want relayed to the entire team. Emma Parker was dead. Cassidy's vision shrank down to a pinpoint as horror pumped through her veins like adrenaline.

A woman she didn't even know had been killed because

someone wanted to kill her. How could a day that had started out so well go so unspeakably wrong?

Cassidy sat staring at her fingers twisted in her lap.

Baker.

Emma had gone to see Airman Baker.

A man discharged over a decade before because Cassidy had snagged him on a gate check. Had he waited all this time to get back at her? He'd been busted for possession. Sure, it had derailed his military career, but it wasn't like the arrest had ruined the guy's life. He'd barely been twenty-one. It wasn't like he couldn't start again after leaving the Air Force.

Something wasn't adding up.

The timing was all off.

Timing.

Jake's warm, broad hand landed on top of hers. A tidal wave of emotion rose inside her. Cassidy bit her lip hard, but she wasn't sure she could outrun it.

While Jake spoke into his phone, she turned to look at the colorful booths as they whizzed past. The explosions had been timed. One per hour. And when they didn't go off as planned, they were capable of being set off at will.

A quick glance down at the phone screen showed the four o'clock hour had come and gone without an explosion on the fairgrounds.

Was it Baker? Had the perpetrator been so busy fending off Emma Parker they hadn't had time to stick to their own deadline? And they were watching her. Waiting for her to break. To try to run away.

Passing her tongue over her front teeth, Cassidy inhaled as she sat straighter. They'd miscalculated. She'd wear their bomb until they blew her sky-high. She'd never give up. Never back down.

"Parker is okay." Jake leaned in closer and gave her clasped hands a gentle squeeze. "It was a stun grenade. They did break the window with a brick, but they tossed the flash-bang in after."

"She bailed?" Cassidy's voice was barely more than a croak.

"She did. Ended up with some bruises from where she hit the pavement. Her car is toast though."

"But she's okay," Cassidy confirmed.

"She's fine."

"Did she see him? Was it Baker?"

"We're getting details thirdhand at this point, but no." Jake gave his head a shake, then shrugged. "They say she didn't get a good look at whoever did the smash-and-blow, but she says she doesn't believe it was Trevor Baker."

"Awfully coincidental to not be him."

Then she remembered the last few words Emma Parker had said before the explosion.

I don't think this is the Baker we're—

Cassidy frowned as she turned the words over in her mind. She couldn't help feeling they'd been on the right track, but they were missing something crucial. Even if Baker had gone after Emma Parker the minute she turned away from the house, he would have had to gather his weapons before following her to her car. It didn't seem probable, but something wouldn't let her scratch Baker off her mental list of suspects entirely.

"But he was home?" she prompted.

He covered his phone and answered her without pulling it away from his ear. "Yes. She said he confirmed his identity when he answered the door." He went back to the call. "When we talk to her again, we need to ask her if he said anything about a brother."

Biting her lip, she turned away as she processed the information. Southwest Little Rock meant he didn't live far from the fairgrounds. It was entirely possible the person who carried out the attack on Agent Parker was nearby.

"Can we get a location on the Baker home?"

One corner of his mouth rose as he held up a finger to ask her to wait as he took in more information. He scribbled something on the edge of the battered paper map, bobbing his head as the person on the other end of the call continued to talk.

Growing impatient, Cassidy unlaced her fingers and shifted to sit on her hands, flattening them beneath her legs and anchoring herself to the bench. The second he ended the call, she pounced.

"Where is the house?"

He gave her a wry smirk. "Over on West 32nd Street."

"West 32nd?" she repeated as she tried to get her bearings. "You mean…" Her words trailing off, she hooked a thumb over her shoulder, momentarily oblivious to the fact they were riding in circles.

"A few blocks west of here. Maybe five minutes' walk?" He blew out a breath. "According to Emma Parker's superior, she's convinced the elder Baker is connected, if not the culprit. They're checking her out at the hospital now, but she wanted to let us know she thinks we're on the trail."

"It's possible for someone to get over to 32nd and back quickly." Cassidy turned the possibility over in her mind. Then she recalled another possibly crucial piece. "They missed four o'clock," she pointed out.

"It's been noted." He heaved a sigh, then scrubbed a hand over his face.

Sensing he was getting ready to leave, she scrambled to get some of her own questioned answered. "Hey, did Bud get the guy from the attractions company yet?"

"Not that I know of," he said, gazing out at the midway.

"I'll nudge him to reach out again," she told him.

Jake grimaced. "I have to get back to the search. Can you document everything you can remember about the Baker case? Make a voice memo if you don't think you can type it into your phone." He sucked in a deep breath then squeezed his eyes shut.

"I have no idea how you're still holding it together on here. This would be killing me."

"Everyone underestimates my stubborn streak."

"Not me." Jake rose and Max clattered to get his paws under him again. "I know exactly how stubborn you can be."

She would have objected to his statement, but he'd already moved to the edge of the platform, preparing to jump. "Hey!" When he turned back, she tried for a stern stare. "Be careful, okay? At this point, I'm willing to let them blow the whole place to pieces, but I don't think I can handle anyone else getting hurt."

"I will," he promised her, his gentle smile reassuring. "Focus on dredging up every little detail you can. At this point, we have no idea what may be useful, so don't leave anything out."

"I won't."

He bent his knees, as if preparing to jump, but then he turned back. "Hey, Cass?"

"Yeah?"

"If you don't care about the property damage, we could get you out of this pack and off this thing," he noted.

She swallowed hard. The same thought popped into her head every few minutes. She could save herself, but then what? Whoever was doing this would still be out there.

Waiting.

Watching.

Willing to strike again at the first opportunity.

Could she live that way? No.

"Yeah, but…if they don't have me, we'll never get them," she pointed out.

He bit down on his bottom lip as if he had to physically repress whatever he wanted to say, then nodded once before taking the leap.

"I'll be back to check in," he declared without so much as a glance over his shoulder.

"You know where to find me." She shrugged, but the joke was wearing as thin as her nerves.

This time she forced herself not to follow his retreating form. Watching him go was torture, and she was getting tired of beating herself up over their situation. She hadn't done anything wrong. Not with Jake. Not with Baker or whoever was doing this. And she was tired of absorbing the hits.

It was time to strike back.

Opening the memo section on her phone, she tapped the little microphone icon and began to speak. When she was done dictating the gist of the story, she stopped the recording and slanted her head back, closing her eyes and trying to conjure the scene. She'd worked in security and law enforcement long enough to know the key to most locked boxes was often lying in plain sight. She needed to relax and try to piece together the whole picture.

She'd traveled back in time to the day she'd first encountered Airman Trevor Baker. She'd had a corporal working with her that day. A trainee. Not new to Security Forces, but new to the base. They were going through the motions. A routine check for ID and guest clearance.

The car was sporty. She'd always been bad at identifying models, but she knew for certain it was a Chevrolet. Newer. Shiny and sleek but outfitted with one of those rumbly exhaust systems designed to draw attention. It had sure caught hers.

Her mobile phone buzzed, jerking her out of the memory.

She looked down at the device in her hand, but the lock screen displayed only a reflection of the sunny weather. Groaning, she reached for her original phone and clicked open the messaging application.

Miss me?

She gave an indelicate snort but didn't bother typing a reply. It vibrated again a second later.

How's life in the fast lane, Lieutenant?

This time, her anger overrode her impulse control. Tapping the reply window, she answered.

I love it here.

The moment the three dots appeared, she regretted engaging with them. The person or people doing this had them running in circles and they knew it. She curled her lips in and bit down as she waited for their response.

Sad to end it. Things are getting fun.

Sitting up, Cassidy typed as fast as she could.

How does this end?

She waited. And waited. But as the minutes passed, it became clear she was not going to get an answer. Ditching the phone for the new one, she placed a call to Jake. He barely got her name out before she started talking.

"Our guy texted," she said without preamble.

"Our guy?" Jake replied, his surprise evident.

"Guy, gal, whatever," she said dismissively. "Asked if I missed them, how I liked the fast lane, used my rank again," she said, feeling breathless. And then a memory caught.

Baker. Or Baker's brother. The guy behind the wheel of the shiny muscle car. His smirky smile. His mocking tone mimicking the formal tone of address Airman Baker had used when answering her questions.

"I think I know," she said, almost speaking to herself.

"Know? Know what?"

"I think I know who we're looking for," she said, her words coming slow as she tried to focus on putting the pieces together.

"You do?"

"I think," she cautioned.

Cassidy curled her fingers into a fist and squeezed as if she could physically hold on to the wisp of certainty she felt when she shifted her attention to Airman Baker's brother. What had his name been? They'd both testified against him in court, but she was having a hard time coming up with the details.

"Cass?" Jake promoted.

"Shh," she snapped, afraid he might scare the supposition away if they didn't approach with caution. "Let me work it all through. I'll call you back."

"Max and I are nearby. We're going to check the Ferris wheel then the kiddie rides, but shout if you come up with anything."

"I will." Ending the call, she cast the phone aside, where it clattered against the other. "Come on, come on." She closed her eyes and willed her memory to cooperate.

Baker's brother. Older, she thought. Cocky. She remembered his smirk clearly. What was his name?

Rather than using precious processing time trying to come up with details, she grappled for the phone again and shot off a voice text to Jake. "Can you get the file Emma Parker had on Trevor Baker? I need to see if there's any mention of his brother in there."

The moment she spoke the words, she recalled Emma saying something about Trevor Baker not being the one they were looking for.

"I think it's the brother. Emma was trying to tell us she suspected Baker's brother," she added to the message before tapping the screen to send it.

She grabbed her radio. "Hey, Bud? Any luck tracking down the manager from the attractions company?"

There was a crackle of static, then Bud Thompson's gruff voice rumbled from the speaker. "On the horn with him now. I'll touch base with you shortly."

"Ten-four."

Running her thumbnail over the plastic ridges of the radio's speaker grill, she tucked her chin to her chest and focused on the toes of her shoes. "Okay…okay. What do we know?"

Speaking the question out loud helped to slot some of the possibilities buzzing around in her brain into place.

They knew whoever was doing this was familiar with her military background.

Their suspect apparently had an ax to grind.

They were dealing with someone who didn't mind waiting to take revenge.

Maybe whoever it was couldn't act on the desire for revenge until now?

She opened the note she'd started dictating and typed "Jail time?" under her account of the security check. Airman Baker had been found guilty of his violations and discharged. His brother had been convicted, she remembered, but what kind of sentence had he served?

She'd called in the local authorities, but since he'd been trying to access a military installation at the time of his arrest, the charges were brought in federal court. She'd been subpoenaed to appear as a witness for the prosecution, but had done nothing more than deliver the facts as to the impetus for the search, seizure and arrest.

She was deep in thought when Bud Thompson pulled alongside the carousel in his cart. He swung his legs out of the vehicle.

"Hey, boss?"

Cassidy turned to look over her shoulder as the platform

spun her around the rear of the ride. She waited for the thud of heavy-soled shoes on the metal deck, but it never came. When she circled back, she waved him in. "Come on up."

She watched as Bud frowned at the painted steeds passing him, as if gauging the speed. Cassidy picked a spot near the control box and counted the seconds until she came around again. She was moving faster than she realized. The horses were definitely moving at more of a gallop rather than a trot.

When she circled again, Bud gave his head a shake. "I don't think I can make it."

"Well, it's gonna be awkward trying to have a conversation like this," she answered, raising her voice as she spun away from him again.

The older man's scowl deepened. Sunlight glinted off the strands of his hair that were more salt than pepper. Then he pulled out his radio. "Let's try this," he suggested, taking a seat on the metal folding chair abandoned by the ride operator.

"Copy." She raised her eyebrows as she sailed by him once more. "Whatcha got?"

"Spoke to Ben Whalen at Continental Attractions. He's down in Florida, of all places. I guess there was an issue with a county fair south of Tampa."

"Did you tell him he has a big problem with a state fair in Arkansas?" she shouted as she went around the bend again.

"I did," Bud assured her. "The guy's pretty squeamish about talking to cops. Colonel Aronson asked me to get what I could out of him."

"And?"

"He said his site supervisor should be on the premises. I asked about controlling the ride and he tells me there's a sort of command center parked somewhere over in RV parking. Says they can do test runs remotely, troubleshoot some of the newer rides, sort of thing. The site supervisor stays there for the duration."

"Do you have eyes on the trailer?"

"Not yet." Cassidy didn't have to see his face to hear his grimace. Bud liked to be the man with the answers. "Whalen told me their company vehicle had to go in the shop. Some issues with hydraulics. Anyway, they rented one for the duration."

Cassidy pursed her lips as she took this information in. "I take it this rental RV has no markings identifying it as the Continental Attractions command center," she said dryly.

"You are correct."

They fell silent for a moment.

Then a new voice broke in. "Did they rent it here or out of state?" Jake asked.

Cassidy sucked in a surprised breath. She'd forgotten Jake had one of their radios clipped to his belt. "O-oh. Good question." When she came around front again, she pointed to Bud and then spoke into the radio. "Most of the vehicles in RV parking should have Arkansas plates."

"I'll check to see if it's in-state or not and let your commander know," Bud promised. "But here's what we found funny… Whalen said he called the site manager earlier and the guy didn't report any issues. Certainly didn't say anything about bombs or explosions."

A cough of disbelief escaped her. "Are you kidding me?" She gaped exaggeratedly at Bud the next time she passed.

"Nope," Bud insisted.

"You have got to be joking," Cassidy said.

There was a short blip of static before Jake broke in again. "What's the site supervisor for the amusement company's name?"

"Hang on." Bud pulled his notebook from his shirt pocket. When she swung past again, she saw him flipping through the pages. "I know I wrote it down," he mumbled. When she flew past him a second time, he was looking up again. "Got it. His name is Troy."

Cassidy repeated the name "Troy" in a whisper. Alarm bells clanged in her head. When Bud came into view again, she clicked the button and demanded, "Is that the guy's first name or last?"

"Oh, sorry," Bud said, juggling his radio and the notebook. "Musta cut out on last one. Troy is his first name. Full name on his employment record is Troy S. Baker."

Chapter Thirteen

"Jake, did you hear—"

He cut her off. "I'm on my way."

When they finished exchanging information with Agent Parker's superior, Colonel Aronson had ordered him to take Max down to inspect the arcade games inside the kiddie section of the midway. But the situation was rapidly unfolding, so Jake made the decision to take a detour.

When he approached the carousel, he found Bud Thompson standing with both feet planted on the ground, his radio clutched in his hand. Gesturing to the blur of color and flash, he asked, "You don't want to ride?"

"I don't have enough spring in my step to be jumping up there at this velocity. I don't even want to think about jumping down," he added.

"I will admit they made it more of a challenge," Jake conceded. "It's easier if you grab a pole and haul up."

"You want to see me getting dragged around like a rag doll," Bud said with a huff.

Jake smiled. "Remind me to send you the GIF of the little girl clinging to the carousel."

Bud cast him a sidelong glare. "I have no idea what you said, but I'm gonna go with 'no, thank you.'"

"If you two are done shooting the breeze," Cass shouted on her next pass.

Jake raised a hand in acknowledgment, then turned to face

the older man. "Will you take the RV information to Colonel Aronson? I want to speak to Cassidy about what we've learned, but…" He pulled a face. "I'm supposed to be working the north end of the arcade games."

Bud gave a huff of a laugh and nodded as he stepped back. "You need a decoy."

"I need a few minutes to talk to Cass, then I'll head straight for kiddie land."

"Fine." Thompson raised his radio and spoke into it. "Captain K-9 is coming up to see you, boss. I'm heading up the hill to fill the honcho in on the RV and Troy Baker," he informed her.

Cass zipped past them again. "Ten-four."

Bud Thompson gave him a jaunty salute before heading for his cart. Jake turned back to the merry-go-round as a cloud blotted out the slanting afternoon sun. The wind kicked up, ruffling Max's fur. He tilted his head back to stare at the sky. The afternoon heat hung on, but big, puffy thunderheads were forming to the west.

"Come on, big guy," he said, giving Max's lead a gentle tug.

He didn't have to ask the dog twice. Max bounded onto the swiftly moving platform as if he did this sort of thing all the time. Jake's landing wasn't quite as graceful. He clung to the brass pole impaling a rearing white stallion until he got his feet under him.

Cass smirked. "I'm going to start scoring people on their mount and dismount."

"Easy for you to say." They threaded their way toward her. "You sit there and the whole world comes to you."

She barked a laugh. "Yeah, it's been super easy to be stuck here in this…horse vortex."

"Horse vortex," he repeated with a laugh.

"Livestock tornado?" she offered.

He gave her a wan smile as he dropped down on the bench

across from her. "You're right. I don't know how you've been able to stand this."

She shrugged. "What's my option?"

Jake inclined his head to concede the point. "I spoke with both Parker and her department head, Simon Taylor. They are following up at the scene, but Trevor Baker is claiming he and his brother fell out years ago. His wife was home at the time of Agent Parker's visit, and confirmed Trevor had not left the house, but said Troy Baker had been harassing them since he was released from prison."

"How long ago?"

"I don't have all the details yet."

"How reliable does Emma think the wife is?"

"Seems good. She's convinced it was the brother."

Cass mulled the information over for a moment, then shook her head. "Something isn't adding up. How would Troy Baker know Agent Parker would go question his brother. And when?"

Jake held his palms up. He was fresh out of theories. "Beats me." He looked down at the two mobile phones on the bench beside her. They were identical, aside from the drop-resistant case on her personal device. "No chance you mixed up phones when calling Parker?"

Cass followed his speculative glance at the phones but shook her head. "No," she insisted. Picking up her original phone, she opened the contacts. "I only have Agent Parker's information saved in the new one. I called from the new phone."

She opened the call log, then turned the screen toward him. Though there were dozens of inbound numbers listed and as many voicemail messages, there hadn't been any outgoing calls placed for hours.

He gnawed the inside of his cheek as he craned his neck to look around. "I wish we knew how he was watching you."

"You and me both, buddy," she answered in a tone dry as dust.

As if her ears were burning, one of the mobiles on the bench lit up with an incoming call from Emma Parker. He watched as Cass snatched the handset and fumbled to accept the call.

"Hey. How are you?"

She sounded breathless and anxious. The urge to take her hand in his again was strong, but he resisted. Instead, he leaned down to pat his dog as Cass switched the call to speaker.

"I have Jake Donovan here with me. And Max."

Emma chortled. "Trooper Max, the wonder dog?"

Jake moved closer to speak into the phone. "The one and only. Hey, did anyone ask you about Airman Baker's brother?"

Emma Parker paused for a moment before answering with caution. "I was going to ask Cassidy about him."

"Did Trevor Baker mention him?"

"Yeah, he mentioned him. He went off on a rant about the guy. Not long out of jail, struggling, coming around Trevor's house saying Trevor owes him and he betrayed him by pleading guilty." She paused for a moment. "Baker's wife doesn't like the brother. Said he's bad news. A narcissist. Always blaming the world for his messes—but particularly blames Trevor. The wife said he's been bothering them."

Jake leaned in. "Did you ask when they'd last seen or heard from him?"

Emma grunted. "No. At first I thought they were trying to deflect, but the more they told me, I did start to wonder."

Intrigued, Cassidy shot Jake a speaking glance. "How was he harassing them?"

"Phone. Texts. Emails. You name it." Emma sighed then continued. "Mrs. Baker said they even bought new phones, but Troy—the brother—got their new numbers." She was quiet for a moment. "We're seriously looking at the brother for this."

"More like staring at him," Jake informed her. "Can you get someone to pull any information we can get on him?"

"I gave one of the guys on my team my notes. I'll pull it all together and get back to you ASAP."

"But aren't you at the hosp—" Cass started to protest, but Parker cut her off.

"I'll be back at my desk within the hour," she announced. And then she ended the call.

"She shouldn't be going to the office. She should be resting," Cassidy insisted.

Jake raised an eyebrow. "Would you?"

She opened her mouth to argue further, quickly snapping it shut. Jake couldn't help but smile when a blush deepened the pink of her wind-chafed cheeks.

"I didn't think so," he said. "Okay, so we have a suspect. We have people digging into his past and we have suspicions concerning his current whereabouts. Do you have any idea why he'd be coming after you so hard?"

Cass pondered the question for a moment, then shook her head slowly. "Not a clue. I mean, I was the one standing beside his car, and I placed the call to the local police, but it certainly wasn't anything personal." She stopped speaking abruptly, the corners of her mouth pulling down. "I mean…this feels personal," she continued, waving an all-encompassing hand. "Ironic. His was one of what was probably a half dozen arrests I either made or assisted with that week. It wasn't personal for me."

"Did you testify in court?"

She nodded. "Here." He watched her tap the phone screen until a soft *swooshing* sound announced a message had been sent. A second later, his own phone chimed.

"I dictated everything I could think of about the stop, the arrest of AFC Baker and the charges brought against his brother." She waited, brows lifted expectantly until he checked his phone.

Jake blinked down at the text filling his phone screen and his stomach somersaulted. "I, uh…" He winced, then pressed the button to exit the screen. "I may have to wait until I have both feet planted on the ground." She chuckled, but there was little mirth in it. In fact, it sounded mildly derisive. His defenses up, he narrowed his eyes. "What?"

She shrugged him off. "Nothing."

"Sounded like something," he quipped.

"Nothing new, I guess." Cassidy brushed his curiosity away with a wave of her hand.

He rocked back until he sat ramrod-straight on the bench. "Now I have to know. What do you want to say to me, Cass?"

"Cassidy." She issued the correction in a tone tinged with acid.

"You clearly have an issue with me," he argued. "Why don't we get it out there now so we can get one with figuring this mess out?"

"One has nothing to do with the other," she countered.

"Indulge me." He practically growled the words at her.

She rolled her eyes, looking like the sassy teenager he'd loved so much back when he was young and had mistaken her sometimes brash behavior as confidence. Now he knew it masked the exact opposite. She was scared. Of course she was. But he was not volunteering to play punching bag for her fear.

"Say it," he challenged.

She threw her hands into the air. "Okay, fine. Somehow you got it in your head you were the wronged party back in the day, but let me remind you, you broke up with me. You were gone, but I stayed right where you left me." She tipped her chin up. "And I see it all so clearly now. We were never moving at the same speed, or in the same space, or wanting things to happen at the same time. Nothing has changed."

"What? How do you figure?" he demanded, as incensed by her annoyance as her assessment. "We were kids, Cassidy."

He placed extra emphasis on using her full name, then immediately regretted it. The snide tone didn't lend much credence to any argument he might make for growing and maturing.

"It doesn't matter," she said, her voice flat.

But her attempt to brush him off only amped up his determination to get his point of view across.

"You were the one who said we should keep things casual," he said.

"You moved to a town three hours away," she reminded him.

"But you were the one who started dating other people."

"I did not," she shot back, her eyes wide with indignation.

"Someone told me you were hanging around with Robby McAvoy."

She blinked and he couldn't tell if she was stunned by the accusation or impressed with his total recall.

"Robby McAvoy?" She said the guy's name like she was parsing it for hidden meaning.

"Yeah."

"Robby McAvoy from Mr. Fenton's history class?" Her brows drew together, thin furrows of hurt creasing her forehead as she stared at him, looking genuinely baffled. He wanted to smooth them away. He wanted to go back. Forget they ever stumbled down this particular path on memory lane.

"Who told you I was dating Robby McAvoy?"

"Jenna—"

"Burke," she chorused along with him. Then, expelling a long sigh of depletion, she gave her head the barest shake. "Of course, Jenna Burke."

"What does that mean?"

The eye roll was back again, but this time her weariness seemed bone deep. "It doesn't matter."

"Yes, it does," he insisted.

She sat straighter, then secured her thumbs under the straps of the backpack and lifted the weight of the bomb she was wearing off her shoulders for a few seconds. "No, it does not. Like Mr. Fenton's class, Jenna Burke and Robby McAvoy, it's history, Jake. It's not what's happening right now."

"I know, but, Cass…"

She held up a hand to stop him. "No. You need to go."

She hooked a thumb over her shoulder, oblivious to the fact she was riding in circles and therefore pointing in all directions. It was abundantly clear that she wanted him to go away.

"Go. There are bombs to be found. And an RV with who knows what waiting for us," she added with a resolute nod.

Jake opened his mouth to object, but she preemptively thrust her palm into his face.

"You can read my ramblings while Max does his thing. I laid it all out there—the stop, the arrests, the testimony I gave. I couldn't remember many of the specifics, but I'm sure your people can fill them in."

"Listen—"

"No, you need to stop dredging up the past and start working because I'd like to have a future. And maybe by the time you get back, we'll figure out how to talk to one another like adults."

"Cass—"

"Jake, I'm not feeling anything near rational at this moment."

He wanted to push back. He wanted to insist she speak her mind here and now so they might figure out what had happened way back then. But Cassidy was right. They had more pressing matters to attend to than a teen romance mired in ancient history.

Without another word, he stood, Max's lead gripped tight in his hand. Max, perceptive boy he was, darted one last worried glance in Cass's direction. Jake could only wonder about what his partner might have seen there, because he would not allow himself to look back.

He and Max hopped down, found their balance on solid ground again, then started up the incline to the fair's main artery. Jake clenched his back teeth, keeping his jaw taut and his eyes moving, taking in everything that lay ahead of them and refusing to indulge in a single backward glance.

The best thing he could do for Cassidy was find a way to

put an end to this madness. And then, once they had Baker or whoever was doing this to her in custody and Cass off that nightmare of a ride…then they would talk it out.

But at the moment, his mind felt cluttered and his emotions chaotic. Cassidy was right; they needed to set their past aside and concentrate on the task at hand. They were closing in on five o'clock and none of the signs they'd found so far were set to the hour. Aronson had put out a call for all available officers to be on the lookout for any indication of where their bomber would strike next.

He needed to stop focusing on why Baker was targeting Cass and figure out a way to get her out of the crosshairs.

True to his word, he headed for the children's rides.

Because the fair was a popular family activity, Kiddie Land made up a decent portion of the midway attractions. Small-scale rides and games where smaller patrons could win small trinkets and stuffed toys. Jake and Max crossed under a colorfully painted archway and made their way to a miniature carousel that featured shiny motorcycles and sidecars.

Hanging back, he gave Max enough lead to move from one shiny cycle to another. While his partner did this thing, Jake turned in a slow circle, taking in his surroundings and searching for any Be Back Soon signs. There wasn't one posted near the operator's stand. He flexed the fingers of his free hand as he swiveled in the opposite direction. If he hadn't been so attuned to the particular shade of sky blue used for the background on the yardstick, he might have missed it. He was smirking at the cutout of a llama warning all riders to wait until the ride came to a complete stop, remembering all the times he'd hopped onto and off a moving carousel in the past few hours.

The warning seemed ridiculous. The kids who were small enough to enjoy these rides were likely too young to read, impervious to safety warnings and accompanied by a parent who wouldn't think twice about jumping off if their kid didn't like the ride. He was about to turn away when he spotted it.

It was thumbtacked to the llama's rear like someone's funny idea of a pin-the-tail game. Jake took a step closer, squinting to be certain he was processing what he saw correctly.

The clock hands were both directed at the twelve. If their theory held true, any explosive on the ride would have already detonated, or wouldn't for hours. He scanned the area again, taking in all the other rides and booths they needed to search, and huffed out a sigh. Clicking his tongue to signal Max, he pushed the button to take up the slack in the retractable leash.

The shepherd turned to him, looking mildly annoyed to have his inspection interrupted.

"Not here." When the dog hesitated, he gave his fingers a snap. Max countered with an impatient whine, Jake rolled his eyes, taking note there were only two more mini motorbikes to be checked out. "Fine. But make it quick."

Figuring they could cover the area faster, Jake released the breakaway on Max's lead as they approached the hot-air balloon ride. "No funny business at the petting zoo," he warned his partner.

Max bounded through the aluminum fencing and went straight to the base of the ride. He watched as Max moved under the arms holding each basket-shaped gondola two feet off the ground. Satisfied his partner was focused on his due diligence, Jake circled the ride, checking for the familiar clock signs. This one was tacked to the front of the operator's control panel with a magnet.

Also set to twelve o'clock.

Jake skipped ahead to a similar setup featuring brightly colored propeller planes. Same sign, same time. He spotted Max trotting across the cable-strewn lane between rides. The fairgrounds were oddly quiet. Sure, every once in a while, a helicopter swooped overhead. And there were more than the usual number of blaring horns up on Roosevelt Road. But the teams were quiet. Only the occasional chirp of radio static cracked the silence on the channel to break the monotony.

The search was on in earnest.

Jake had no doubt his fellow officers were as sick of this game as he and Cass were. They'd been at it all afternoon, and the sense they were looking for what could be a needle-size bit of plastic explosive in a carnival-colored haystack was not lost on anyone.

By the time he approached the twirling apple ride, his dog was giving a bench near a miniature roller coaster with cars painted to look like the segments of a caterpillar a thorough sniff. Jake made a mental note to check the signs posted near each of those rides on their way back to the center of the action.

He and Max made it all the way through the toddler rides and were working through the line of less-challenging arcade games when a crackle of static undercut the song Jake had been whistling tunelessly.

"Ten minutes until five. Fall back," Aronson ordered.

Jake turned away from the last two booths, muttering as he reattached Max's leash. "We're getting forty minutes out of every hour. Less, with informational meetings."

"You'd have more time to work if you spent less time 'checking' on Ms. Walker," Colonel Aronson chastised. "And move your mic lower on your vest and turn your radio up. You keep unintentionally keying in."

Heat rose in Jake's cheeks. "Ten-four. Sorry, sir. Didn't realize it was me."

Aronson's response was brusque. "Come up here. I want to run something past you."

Jake yanked the radio clip from his vest and glared at it as if it had purposefully set out to make him look the fool. But as he reattached it to one of the loops, he looked down and found his partner staring up at him.

The dog's sympathy was more than he could stand.

Jake narrowed his eyes at the dog. "No, don't look at me like that. If you wanna give me a hard time like the rest of the guys, cool. But don't go all pity puppy on me."

The colonel's jibe and previous admonitions played in a loop in the back of his mind, but they couldn't stop his feet from veering in the direction of the carousel. He and Max approached, skirting the fencing outside the spinning Round-Up ride and cutting across the area set up below the Ferris wheel.

Any trepidation he might have felt about taking the detour dissipated when Cass lifted a hand in greeting. He smiled as she spun away from him. He picked up his pace, determined to have a few words with her before he retreated up the hill to the arena.

Jake was almost past the ride's waiting area when he caught sight of something familiar. Tacked to a red-and-black warning sign listing the rules Ferris wheel riders were expected to adhere to was a Be Back Soon sign.

It's clock hands were set to five o'clock.

Chapter Fourteen

"Chief, I think we have another."

Instinctively, Jake turned his head from side to side, grateful to have someone else confirm what he thought he was seeing. But the call had come over the radio.

No one was there with him. Maybe he was seeing things?

Jake turned back to the Ferris wheel, locking onto the sign once again. Someone droned on about finding something at the dining area across from the main stage, but Jake could barely take in the information. Blinking rapidly, he tried to process what he was seeing. And hearing. A blast of chatter came through on the radio and things clicked into place.

Two bombs. They'd located two bombs, but only one of them was marked for imminent detonation.

His heart hammering, he spoke, cutting across the other transmissions. "Sir, I have five o'clock."

There was a prolonged pause, then Aronson came on the channel. "Yes, almost five o'clock. Everybody fall back. Now!" He barked the last word with enough urgency to snap Jake's momentary paralysis.

He and Max took off toward the carousel at a trot. "No, sir. I mean I have eyes on the sign. It's posted at the Ferris wheel."

"Fall back, Donovan," Aronson ordered again. "We'll deal with whatever you've found after the top of the hour."

Jake didn't break stride. Nor did he change direction. If there was a bomb planted at the Ferris wheel, Cass was too close for comfort. She needed to take cover.

"Come on, boy." Jake and Max prepared to leap onto the spinning ride. His feet landed with thud loud enough to make her head swivel. Their gazes met, and they both started talking.

"You need to get down," he told her.

"Troy Baker was released two months ago."

"Get down," he repeated. "Now."

Breath coming fast and heavy, he reached the bench where she sat perched on the edge. When she didn't move, he stepped into her space, closed his hand around her upper arm and pulled her from the seat.

"Hey," she cried when her knees hit the corrugated metal.

"Bomb," he growled into her ear as he lowered himself on top of her.

Cass craned her neck and snarled at him, but he didn't care. The only thing that mattered was her safety. All he wanted was the chance to talk to her once all this was over.

"There's a bomb between us," she reminded him in a voice dripping with acid.

"The Ferris wheel is set to blow at—"

Before he could finish the sentence, the explosion split the still evening wide open.

The flash. The bang. The acrid smell of accelerant followed by a hailstorm of dirt and debris. He held her down until the last bits of fallout dropped. Then, as he was pushing up on his hands to let her rise, a bone-chilling screech rang out.

"What the—" He looked up as they spun past.

The bomb had been placed under the Ferris wheel's landing platform and had blown out the rear of its base. He should have been relieved to see the blast pattern had spewed away from the midway, but he was too horrified by what he didn't see.

One of the wheel's rust-speckled support posts was missing.

There was a creak. A groan. Then the enormous wheel seemed to hunker down and keel over.

Jake squeezed his eyes shut as he realized the top of the ride would land on the carousel.

Cassidy reared up in a futile attempt to push him off her, before he flung his full body weight onto her once more.

"Jake!" she yelped, indignant.

But there was no time to argue. And no chance of jumping. The best they could do was hang on and hope they were on the opposite side when it hit them. The creaks and groans gave way to distressed shrieks as gondolas wobbled wildly and rivets popped, setting spokes welded into place years, if not decades before, free.

"Wha—" Cass gasped as an unholy screech sang out.

"It's coming down! Just stay down, Cass!"

He pressed his face into her hair and covered his helmeted head and hers with both arms. The structure hit the canopy with a tooth-jarring crash. All around them, horses sprang from their tethers. Bits of gilt and glass shattered. The metal platform tipped and tilted. Gears ground. The carnival-painted top dipped precariously as the motor worked to push through the obstacle. The hiss of hydraulic release drowned out most of the other noises. The whole contraption shook and shuddered as it strained.

And at last, the crippled carousel ground to a halt.

They lay there in stunned stupor. Unfolding his arms, Jake brushed pieces of splintered sparkly wood from her hair.

"Are you okay?" His voice was hoarse from either the smoke rising around them or strain. Maybe both.

"Yeah…" It was clear from her shaking voice she was reassuring herself as much as him.

He licked dry lips, then chanced a glance at the debris all around them.

The wreckage struck ahead of the bench where she'd been

sitting. The canopy top was now tilted at a rakish angle, its edge a mere two feet higher than a seahorse's head. If they hadn't ducked, it would have knocked them to the floor.

A plume of dark, acrid smoke billowed in from the platform of the Ferris wheel. Another, scented with the stench of burning rubber, seeped out from the carousel's center column. He coughed, but it was impossible to take in any good air.

"We have to go," he said, scrambling up from his prone position.

"But I—" She pushed her hair back from her face as she rocked back onto her knees. "He said—"

"We're done letting him call the shots," Jake snapped. "This is coming off," he added, looping his hand under one of the straps of the backpack.

"But, Jake—" Cassidy started to protest, but whatever words she had were translated into a yelp when he dragged the straps of the pack down her arms.

"All bets are off," he growled. "We have to get you off this thing. It could catch fire, bomb or no bomb. We have to go."

"But what if they see us taking it off?"

He tugged the pack off her and flung it into the tangle of Ferris wheel wreckage mere feet away from them. "Hopefully, the wreckage took out the cameras. If they can't see you, they won't detonate." He pulled her to her feet and propelled her to the edge of the platform. "Now, run!"

"But we have to—"

He grabbed her hand and pulled her down off the platform. "We have to get clear."

Cassidy stumbled against him as she landed, her legs buckling. "We can't just take off. Look at this." Her voice rose as she gestured wildly to the destruction. "He's not going to let me go, Jake. He has me in his sights and he has nothing to lose."

Jake stepped forward, cupped her elbow and gave her a gentle but insistent tug. "Then we need to get to him before he can get to you."

"Wait, I need my phones." She groped around on the debris-strewn bench, tears from the smoke streaming from her eyes.

Then realization hit him full in the chest. Time slowed. So did his movements. For a moment. He stared at Cass, flexing his jaw as if testing whether it would hold or not, then whirled in a circle, head swiveling from side to side.

"Whoa there," she said, brow puckering. "We stopped spinning and you want to start all over again?"

"Where's Max?"

He snapped his fingers and let out a short, sharp whistle.

But Max did not come.

Cassidy dropped to her knees amid the wreckage they'd shaken off. "Here he is."

Jake closed the gap between them in two long strides. Blinking rapidly and waving his hand to disperse some of the smoke, he peered over her shoulder and found his dog tucked under one of the benches. Max blinked blearily but made no move to crawl out from his hiding place.

"Come on, boy." Jake reached for him, but his partner recoiled. "We have to get off this thing."

She bit her lip as she stroked his partner's fur. When she spoke, her tone was calm but urgent. "Jake, I think he's hurt."

He crowded into the cluttered space, gently urging her to move aside. When she pushed up onto one of the benches, he slipped into her spot and looked deep into Max's dazed amber eyes.

"Hey, bud." He ran a hand along the dog's back and flank. Max flinched and bared his teeth when Jake's hand grazed something sharp protruding from his hind leg. "Oh no." His heart lodged firmly in his throat.

Max was his partner. They lived together. Ate together. Depended on one another. And he'd failed to keep him safe.

The dog blinked lazily, then rested his huge muzzle on his front paws again.

"Oh, buddy, I'm sorry," he crooned as he slid his hand back up the shepherd's back, looking for the lead attached to his vest. "I'm gonna get you out of here," he promised.

The sound of running footfalls and motorized vehicles filled the eerie aftermath. The cavalry was coming, but he needed to make sure Cass was away from the area before their bomber figured out she'd slipped free of his trap. And he had to get Max out into an area where he could check his wound.

Glancing around wildly, he spotted her blazer. "Can I borrow your jacket?" He nodded toward her. "I need to muzzle him so I can l lift him."

Cass shrugged out of the jacket. "Muzzle him? Are you afraid he'll bite you?"

"He's hurt and in pain. I'd bite anyone who tried to move me, too," he said, speaking in a reassuring lilt meant to soothe both woman and dog. "Toss it to me, then jump down. Try to stay toward the back of the ride until we can scope out who's out there."

To his relief, she didn't argue with him. He heard the slap of her feet hitting asphalt. Slipping the jacket over his dog's head, he spoke in a firm tone as he slid one of the sleeves up over the shepherd's powerful jaws. "Only for a minute, buddy."

The dog's growl of displeasure dissolved into a keening whimper as Jake slid his arms under Max's lax body and rolled him up against his chest. Bracing their combined weight against the bench opposite, he levered himself onto his feet, holding his ninety-pound partner in his arms.

"Hope you had fun while it lasted," he huffed as he shuffled to edge. "We're never riding one of these things again."

Max let out a yip when Jake stepped down onto solid ground as gracefully as he could. "I know. I know," he huffed consolingly. "I'm so sorry."

He turned toward the rear of the ride and found Cass waiting for him. She'd positioned herself between two of the trailers holding massive generators, her back against one wall, as she swept the vicinity with worried, wary eyes.

"You made it," she cried as he approached.

"We made it," he said to the dog as he bent to lower Max to the ground at Cass's feet. The moment he slid his arms out, he plucked the jacket off the dog's head. "I'm sorry," he said again, apologizing for both the injury and the indignity.

Max tipped his head back, staring at Cass. Jake couldn't blame him. Filthy, bruised and bedraggled as she was, seeing her without the pack strapped to her back was the best thing he'd seen all day.

"Hey." She dropped to one knee beside Max's head. "Such a good boy," she said, reaching out to stroke the black stripe on the top of his head. "So brave."

"He always gets the girl." Jake was unable to suppress his smile as he said it. If he was going to lose Cassidy's heart to anyone, he preferred it be Max.

Jake checked the dog over, running gentle hands through thick fur. He grimaced when he spotted the piece of mirrored glass lodged in his partner's upper leg. "I'm going to get you fixed up."

He patted down his vest pockets. When he found a treat and offered it to Max on his palm, the dog sniffed it, then turned his nose up. "Boy, you are hurt," Jake said as he put the morsel back in his pocket. "Okay, we need an EMT."

"I'll get one."

Cassidy started to rise, but he caught her wrist. "No. I think you should keep a low profile. Let him wonder if you're trapped in there." He jerked his head in the direction of the wreckage.

She shook her head, the familiar stubborn gleam back in her eyes. "I'm not hiding out, waiting for this thing to be over. If he wants me, he'll have to come and get me." She shrugged off his grip and rose. "Besides. We can't let anyone near this mess. Someone," she enunciated, pinning him with a glare, "tossed a backpack full of explosives into the mix."

Jake winced, then nodded. "Okay, fine. We need to clear the area."

"You, too," she pointed out.

As if he'd grown tired of being left out of the conversation, Max rolled onto his belly, stretching his front paws out as if preparing to rise. But when he attempted to get his hand legs under him, he subsided with a whimper of pain.

Jake heaved a sigh. "I'm gonna have to carry you, bud. It's gonna hurt, and I need you to promise not to rip my face off," he said, moving into a squat beside his partner.

"Do you want my jacket back?" Cassidy offered the wadded ball of fabric.

Jake shook his head and looked into Max's eyes. "Nah. I think we'll be okay without it. He can see better now, can't you, boy?"

He groaned as he heaved the dog into the cradle of his arms once more. Max's tongue lolled out of the corner of his mouth, and he began to pant rapidly. "I'm going to have to cut back on your treats," he grumbled as they followed Cass out from behind the wreckage, picking through the ground littered with cables and detritus from the blast.

He spotted Colonel Aronson talking to Bud Thompson as soon as they rounded the corner. The older man stood scowling at the twisted metal of the Ferris wheel and the carousel's collapsed canopy.

"Sir?"

Aronson pivoted on his heel, his expression lighting with relief when he spotted Cass walking beside him. "You're out."

"We are."

Jake was winded by exertion, so Cass took over.

"Max is hurt. There's a piece of glass in his leg and he's dazed from the explosion," she said in a rush.

Bud flipped the rear seat of his golf cart down. "Put him on the cart."

Aronson pointed one blunt finger at her. "Where's the backpack?"

"In there," she said, pointing to the approximate location. "Jake figured this area is already a wreck and so we…" She shrugged. "Jake thought it best that we ditch it."

As Jake deposited his injured partner on the rear deck of the cart, Aronson raised a bullhorn to his mouth. "Fall back. Fall back. Undetonated device in the area."

There was a flurry of action as the men and women who usually rushed into danger hurried to escape it.

Bud gestured to Cassidy. "You take it. I'll meet you up there."

"Thanks," Jake said. He climbed onto the passenger seat and knelt, throwing his arms across Max to hold him in place. They took off with a jolt and soon they were speeding up the path toward Barton Coliseum.

Max was looking more alert when they coasted to a stop in front of the arena doors. One of the fire department ambulances pulled in from the opposite direction. Evan Furst hopped down and jogged over to the cart. "Got a call someone is injured," he said, eyes darting from Cassidy to Jake and back again.

"It's Max," he said, gesturing to the dog's leg.

Furst didn't miss a beat. He waved one of the paramedics who'd been riding in the passenger seat over. "Looks like he took a bit of shrapnel," Furst observed, offering his knuckles for Max to sniff.

Jake appreciated the other man's matter-of-fact tone. He'd been so relieved to get Cass out of the awful situation she'd been trapped in, he'd forgotten about his best friend. Guilt gnawed at him. He lowered his head to look into Max's eyes. "I'm sorry," he said for what felt like the thousandth time.

The EMT opened a field bag and pulled out a sturdy pair of tweezers. "I've got you, Trooper." He spoke directly to Max. Turning his attention to Jake, he said, "Hey, I'm Russell. My sister is a vet. I'm going to call her, and we'll get him fixed up." He pulled his mobile from his pocket and speed-dialed a number. The moment a woman answered, Russell jumped in without preamble. "Can dogs have lidocaine?"

She hummed noncommittally. "Is there a particular reason you're asking or is this knowledge you need for *Jeopardy!*?"

Jake watched as the guy pulled a pair of sterile gloves from the bag. "I have a K-9 officer injured, a German shepherd by the name of—" He looked to Jake.

"Max."

"Trooper Max has a piece of glass or mirror embedded in the upper part of his leg. Can I numb the area?"

His sister didn't miss a beat. "Anterior or posterior?"

"Posterior," Russell provided. "Closer to his rump."

"Good. Lower risk it hit an artery," she said. "Dosing a dog can be tricky. If he'll let you remove it without anesthetic, it would be safer for him."

Russell raised his brows at Jake, who nodded. "He'll hold."

"Do you have a muzzle handy?" the vet asked.

When the paramedic looked to him again, he gave his head a sharp shake. "I can use his leash, but he won't bother you. Not as long as he knows I'm here."

"Better use the leash, in case. Never know how an animal in pain will react," Russell's sister said, her tone gentle, but firm.

Jake leaned in and pressed his forehead to Max's for a moment. "This is only to make them feel better. I know you're a tough guy."

As if he understood, Max raised his head enough for Jake to wrap the leash around his muzzle twice.

"Okay, we're secured," Russell said into the phone. "Remove the glass?"

"Yes. Treat him like you would a human patient from here on out. Let me know if you think he'll need stitches."

The man pressed a pack of gauze into Cass's hands. "I'll need this to apply pressure."

"On it." She tore into the sterile pack.

"Okay, here we go," the medic said, meeting Jake's eyes.

"Don't think about it too much. Get it out," his sister advised. "If by chance the bleeding doesn't slow or looks to be arterial, use the leash as a torniquet."

To Jake's relief, the man didn't hesitate. Max let out a sharp keening whine when Russell plucked the thin shard of mirror from the wound, subsiding the moment the dressing was pressed against the wound.

"Doesn't appear to be too deep," the medic said. "Three millimeters, maybe?"

"If the bleeding slows on its own, clean and dress, wrapping the bandage snug around the leg to close the wound. Meet me at the clinic, and I'll take it from there."

This time, Jake spoke directly into the phone. "We have no idea how long we'll be here."

Max blew out a billowy breath, the picture of patience and forbearance. Jake chuckled, rubbing the dog's ears as he removed the strap from Max's muzzle.

"We can't bring him in right now, Jeannie. He's a detection officer and we're at an active crime scene."

There was only a moment's pause on the other end, but the timbre of the vet's voice told him she understood what wasn't being said. No doubt, she'd seen or heard some of the news coverage by now. "Send me a couple of pictures before you dress the wound," she instructed Russell. "He should be okay. Dogs are remarkably resilient. No doubt Max is humoring y'all at this point."

Jake chuckled at her fairly accurate assessment. "I like being humored."

The whooshing sound of a text being sent jerked him back to reality. He looked over in time to see Russell reapplying pressure with the gauze pad. A second later, his sister spoke again. "Looks okay. Wash it out with saline or Betadine, cover and wrap it. If he's in too much pain, call me back and we'll figure out what you can give him. No anti-inflammatories. Call me when y'all wrap up and we'll take a closer look."

Jake blew out a relieved breath as Russell started pulling supplies from his bag. "Thank you both."

"My pleasure. Catch me up later, Russ," she ordered. Then three short beeps indicated the end of the call.

"Well, she was handy," Jake said as he watched Russell cleanse the wound. "Glad you were nearby, Russell."

"Me, too." The other man shrugged but didn't pause in his work. When he was done, he ran his hand soothingly over Max's flank. "And this guy is a trooper. Maybe I won't be so offended the next time Jeannie calls me a dog."

Chapter Fifteen

Cassidy watched as the officers from various agencies filed back up the hill. Colonel Aronson brought up the rear of the reluctant retreat. She stroked Max's soft fur as the dog lay panting over a collapsible bowl filled with fresh water. As far as she was concerned, the golf cart was all his. Bad knees and bunions were no longer a valid excuse; Bud would have to hoof it for a while.

"Colonel," Jake said as the older man approached. "What's the situation down there?"

"Fire department is coating the place in foam," he said in a brusque tone. "On the upside, we have twelve devices accounted for. By my count, we have seven detonated, four located, one disarmed."

She watched as Jake tallied the devices up in his head then nodded. "Yes."

"You just had to throw backpack in there," the colonel groused.

Jake grimaced and Cassidy felt compelled to rush into the fray. "It was my idea," she said, but the claim sounded false even to her own ears. "I mean I agreed with Agent Donovan. The area was already torn up, so there was no point in carrying it to another location."

Colonel Aronson shook his head in the affirmative. "You are correct. It means we'll have to wait for our friend to set it off though."

"Not if we find him first," Jake said, rolling off the cart onto his feet. "We suspect he's been holed up in the amusement company's command post over in the RV park."

"I doubt he's still there," Aronson said.

"If he isn't, there may be clues as to where he would go," Cassidy chimed in. "But I have a feeling he hasn't bailed yet."

Colonel Aronson turned to look at her, eyes narrowing. "Why do you say that?"

"Has he texted?" Jake demanded, speaking over his superior.

"What? No." Cassidy wagged her head, but a pang of guilt shot through her. "I don't know."

She hadn't even thought to check the mobile phones she'd retrieved from the rubble. The moment they'd seen Max was hurt, everything else had fallen by the wayside. She extracted the devices from the pocket of her rumpled blazer.

She had unread messages on both.

Cassidy's hands shook as she opened her personal cell. The first message read simply:

You'd better be on that ride.

Then there was another sent two minutes after the first.

I mean it. You move, I blow this thing.

She handed Jake the phone, incredulous. "Does he really think I'll continue to sit there with the whole thing falling down around me?" She waved an arm in the general direction of the midway. "You were right. There's no way for us to salvage this."

"But now we know he lost track of you. We also know he's triggering the devices manually." He surveyed their immediate vicinity. "We have four active IEDs on site," Jake reminded her. "And a guy who has an ax to grind running loose around here."

"Yeah, well, I've had enough," Cassidy announced. She marched back to the cart.

"What are you going to do?" Jake asked.

"I'm going to start searching the RVs," she said, plucking the heavy light from its holster. Dropping into the driver's seat of the golf cart, she swiveled to look back at Jake and Max. "I'm taking the cart."

The lines bracketing Jake's mouth deepened when he frowned. "I don't know if—"

But she cut him off by twisting the key. Reaching down, she switched the toggle to put it into Reverse. A high, hollow warning signal proclaimed her intention to back up. She quirked an eyebrow at Jake when he made no move to remove himself or take his dog from the rear deck.

"You guys coming with me?"

"Cass, you can't go running off—"

"Watch me."

She pressed the brake to the floorboard then released it. The cart began to roll without so much as a tap to the accelerator. The group assembled behind them scattered like chickens. She stomped the brake and the cart jerked to a halt.

"It could be dangerous," he argued.

"All the bombs are up here," she said, waving an arm out in front of her.

"I'm not talking about the bombs. I'm talking about the bomb*er*," he countered.

"You think he's sitting around waiting for someone to come a-knocking?" she scoffed. When he made no move to get off the cart, she tried to reason with him. "It's more likely we'd catch him roaming around the wreckage. I haven't answered his texts. He'll want to get a closer look."

Jake swore softly under his breath, but she felt no triumph in winning this round. His jaw flexed, the little muscle in the corner twitching with tension, as he stared off in the direction of the east parking lots. At last, he blew out a gusty breath and said, "I'm coming with you."

Cassidy blinked, surprised by his decision. "What about Max?"

"He's coming, too." Jake wrapped one hand around the canopy support, then hooked the other under Max's harness.

"But he's hurt," she argued.

"Even hurt, he'll be an asset to us."

She glanced back, but Max only returned her stare, remarkably bright eyed. Darting a glance at Colonel Aronson, she asked, "Shouldn't you check to see where they need you?"

He busied himself with checking Max's bandage. "They have plenty of coverage for the three sites they can access. I'm thinking he'll keep everyone away from the midway for now."

"What if our guy is skulking around there?"

"I'm sure he'll secure the perimeter and have the fire department continue to monitor for flare-ups." He flashed a wry smile. "But I tossed an undetonated device into the mess, remember? I'm not going to presume to tell the colonel how to handle his scene. I'm probably not at the top of his list of favorite people right now."

She chanced another peek at the stern-faced commander. "Taking off might be a one-way ticket to the bottom."

"Not if we find something to help us grab this guy." His expression melted into a grim smirk. "I'm already in the doghouse, Cass. Maybe, if we can get a bead on this guy, I won't be busted down to highway patrol when this is all over."

Her heart squeezed. She could see genuine worry in his eyes, but also the steely glint of determination. Jake Donovan had worked his way up the ranks of his chosen profession, and he'd put it all on the line because some madman had decided he wanted to take her out.

She flipped the switch to put the cart into Drive. Then she handed him both of her mobile phones and said, "If you're coming along for the ride, make yourself useful," before punching the accelerator.

They zipped down the concrete path leading to the rear of the arena, then down the opposite side of the hill. The east parking areas of the fairgrounds were reserved for exhibitor and vendor trailers and RVs. They were crammed into the narrow lot bumper to bumper. From this vantage point, Cass thought it looked as packed as a dealership lot. She let off the pedal as they approached the end of the walkway.

"Bump," she warned as she approached the transition from concrete to grass.

"Got it." He let out an exaggerated grunt and held on to Max as they rolled over the uneven terrain.

"I'm gonna head to the south end and work my way north," she said, shouting over her shoulder to be sure he heard her over the noise of the cart.

"I'll keep an eye out for any out-of-state tags or vehicles that look like they may be a rental."

"Good idea," she shouted. "A lot of the local farms and operations will put their logos somewhere on the vehicle. It doesn't sound like the amusement company bothered to take the time."

"Agreed." Jake leaned over the seat and pointed to a shiny new RV. "I'm guessing a rental will likely be a newer model."

Cassidy let off the gas and turned to shoot him a smile. "You're smarter than you look, Donovan."

"You don't think I look smart?"

"Seems unfair is all," she said with a cavalier shrug.

"How so?"

"To be smart and pretty," she said as they coasted to a halt beside the large RV.

There were no markers indicating it belonged to one of the local ranchers or any of the myriad other businesses that supplied the fair. When she glanced back over her shoulder, she found Jake staring at her intently. "What?"

"Sounds suspiciously like flirting, Cassidy Walker."

"I'm not sure you'd know the flirting if you heard it, Donovan," she answered and slid from the driver's seat. "I'm going to go check this tag."

Jake pulled his phone from his belt and slid off the rear deck of the cart. He gave Max a firm pat and a gentle command. "Stay."

As he followed her around to the back of the bus, he said, "Did Bud ask them to send over the rental agreement?"

"I'm sure he did, but I don't think we've seen it yet."

"It should have the make, model and at least a VIN on it, if not a plate number."

Cassidy pivoted in his direction and tapped her temple. "You're getting smarter by the second, Donovan."

"Does mean I'm getting prettier, too?"

Cassidy spotted an Arkansas plate as well as a bumper sticker with a rearing horse that read, "Hey! Ho! We're Off to the Rodeo."

She turned to return to the front of the vehicle and ran smack into Jake's chest. "Oof!"

He caught her upper arms and held her steady, making sure her feet were planted beneath her before loosening his grip. "Okay there?"

"I'm fine. It's hard to believe the earth is still spinning after being stuck on ride for so many hours. Hardly feels like it's moving at all," she said, attempting a weak smile.

"You're going to have to get used to gravity again, and life without excessive g-forces. You might as well be an astronaut," he added with a wry smile.

She took a quick step back. A chill raised over her arms the second the warmth of his hands was gone. Still feeling unsteady, she groped for better equilibrium. "Arkansas tags," she blurted. "There's also a rodeo bumper sticker. Looks like we have a bronc rider."

He tipped his head in the direction at the door, "Should we give it a knock?"

"We evacuated most of the people staying on site."

"Can't hurt to try," he said, striding too the door. He rapped on it sharply then stepped back, his hands coming to rest on his hips.

Standing behind him, Cassidy eyed the sidearm he wore and felt an instant flood of relief he'd decided to come along on this search. The lot felt abandoned. Away from the bustle of first responders, this corner of the sprawling fairgrounds felt desolate. Since the explosion, an eerie tension had settled over the area.

They got no answer, and the door was securely locked.

She glanced over both shoulders, then hooked a thumb toward the cart. "Let's take a moment to regroup." Without waiting for his reply, she strode back to the driver's seat and slid onto it.

She gave Max a gentle pat. "How you doing, huh?"

For his part, the German shepherd seemed markedly improved. His ears were up, his eyes bright, and an enormous pink tongue lolled out the side of his mouth as he surveilled their surroundings.

"Doing better?"

"He looks better," Jake said as he approached. He checked the dog's bandage, ruffled his ears, then leaned down to look his partner square in the eyes. "You're good, right? Wanna help us look for the bad guy?"

As if he understood every single word they said, Max let out a single, startlingly loud bark.

Jake gave the dog's neck a reassuring stroke. "You're one heck of a trooper, Trooper Max."

"Yes, he is," Cassidy agreed.

But rather than climbing up onto the deck with the dog, Jake gathered her abandoned mobile phones and moved to the passenger side. The whole cart dipped under his weight as he climbed aboard. She said nothing as she took both phones back from him. "Too bad you're not a very good assistant."

"I was too busy holding on to Max and trying not to fall off the back of this thing to look at either of them."

"Fine." She sounded petulant but had a hard time caring about her tone. When he let out a chuckle, she shot him an exasperated glare. "I have to tell you I wouldn't mind if I never read another text message again," she said, her tone edged with apprehension.

"I don't blame you." He reached over and pulled her personal phone from her hand. "Tell you what, I'll check this one if you'll see if there's any good information on the other one."

Cassidy exhaled her relief and bobbed her head in a grateful nod. "Thanks."

"My pleasure."

She couldn't resist watching out of the corner of her eye as he keyed in the code to unlock the phone. There were nearly two dozen new text notifications. Most appeared to be from people in her stored contacts, but more than a handful were from unknown numbers.

He started opening them, muttering under his breath as he read, "Reporter. Reporter. Someone named Suzette."

He raised an eyebrow and she shrugged. "No idea."

"Probably another reporter. This one looks like a food vendor. And somebody named Kevin saw what's happening on the news and wants to know if you're okay," he said, enunciating each word pointedly.

The jealous tinge to his tone warmed her cheeks. "Kevin? The only Kevin I know is my cousin on my dad's side," she informed him.

"Came up as an unknown number," he commented.

"We're not close. Obviously," she added with a laugh.

Jake fell silent as he perused the rest of the messages. "Nothing here from our guy," he said at last.

Cassidy nodded and looked down at the phone in her hand. "I dread dealing with the fallout from all of this." She scrolled through the accumulated missed calls and messages. "Not putting things back together, so much as having to talk to the reporters and all that stuff," she said with an offhand wave.

Jake hummed in his throat. "A double-edged sword. Feed them a little and they go into a frenzy. Don't feed them at all and they speculate."

"Oh, Emma Parker called," she said, looking over at him. Her thumb moved to hit the redial button before the words finished leaving her mouth. Placing the call on speakerphone, the two of them bent closer together as they listened to it ring through.

"Parker here. Is that you, Cassidy?"

"It's me."

"Oh, thank goodness." Agent Parker exhaled, clearly relieved. "We got word of what happened with the Ferris wheel, but I couldn't get a clear answer on whether you were on or off the carousel."

"There's a reason for that," Cassidy said.

"Ah, got you," Emma Parker replied. "Well, I'm glad to hear you're okay."

"Makes three of us." Cassidy asked, "Are you feeling all right?"

"I'm banged up, but mostly from bailing and tripping over my own feet," Emma said, her tone dry as dust. "My fiancé is with me now, and things are much better. Did they pass the information I gathered along to you?"

"Yes, and I think you're absolutely right." She and Jake exchanged a look and he placed a cautioning hand on her arm.

"We don't know who's listening," he whispered.

She nodded to him, then refocused on the conversation. "Yeah, right. Yes, the information was helpful, and I think it's setting us on the right path," Cassidy confirmed.

Emma caught on quickly. "Some of my team have been interviewing people in the neighborhood, and one of the neighbors reported seeing a man dressed in a dark T-shirt and utility pants running away from the scene."

Cassidy hummed. "What was Airman Baker wearing when you stopped by to interview him?"

"Gray gym shorts and a red Razorbacks shirt," Emma recalled.

"And the timing?" Cassidy wondered if it was within the realm of possibility for Trevor Baker to have changed his clothes between the time of Emma's exit from his home and the brick being thrown through the car window.

"Impossible. He and his wife were at the door as I was leaving," Emma told them.

Jake leaned in closer. "Has anyone followed up with Baker to see if he noticed the person who approached your vehicle?"

"Yes, but both he and his wife claim they were back inside by the time the incident took place."

"Would have been too easy," Cassidy said, her lips curling up in a mirthless smile.

"True. Then again, I'm not entirely sure Trevor Baker would have been completely truthful even if he'd seen something."

"I thought they were estranged?" Cassidy pressed.

"They are, but blood being thicker than water and all. I think Trevor feels guilty his brother's life has been derailed." Emma took a deep breath and exhaled slowly. "But I have a hunch, and it's strictly a hunch, that his brother may not feel the same way."

"Why do you think that?"

"Because a police officer was attacked outside of Trevor Baker's home. He may have been trying to set his brother up to look like the guilty party."

"Trevor testified against Troy as part of his plea deal," Cassidy murmured.

"Bingo," Emma Parker replied. "And there's your motive."

Chapter Sixteen

The moment they ended the call, Jake radioed the colonel and asked him to meet them at the entrance to the RV lot. Minutes later, the man came striding down the hill, an assortment of uniformed techs following in his wake. "Tell me everything we know," he demanded as they approached.

Jake smirked. "Not a tall order at all."

But Cassidy didn't hesitate. She launched right into "Troy Baker was the older brother of Airman Trevor Baker, the gentleman Agent Parker interviewed this afternoon." She didn't need to add anything about the attack. "I encountered the brothers one day when I was on duty at the base. We had the usual Sunday-afternoon backup at the gates to the base, so they called in extra Security Forces officers to help with clearance. I had a trainee working with me that day. I don't recall his name, but I know he was green. Baker's car was six or seven cars back from the checkpoint, but I could see one of the occupants was in uniform, so likely active duty coming back onto base. I thought it would be an easy pass, but I was wrong."

The colonel nodded. "How did it go sideways?"

"They were arguing when we approached the car. Airman Baker wanted to get out and walk in, but for some reason his brother, Troy, was not having it." She frowned as she cast her mind back. "I don't recall his reasoning, but when we engaged with Airman Baker, it was apparent he was impaired."

"Drunk?"

"We could smell alcohol, yes. But it was more his demeanor tipped us off. He was cagy. I'd even go so far as to say paranoid. He produced his identification and paperwork showing he had leave, but it ended at noon, and it was well past two when we spoke to him."

"He was AWOL," Aronson concluded.

"Technically, yes, he was. When I informed him of his status, he became defensive and belligerent. I asked him to step out of the vehicle. His brother finally spoke up, telling him he didn't have to do what I told him to do, et cetera." She waved a hand as if the rest of the exchange was not important. "We eventually placed Trevor Baker under arrest for various violations. When we patted him down, we found he was carrying narcotics onto base. The brother, Troy Baker, made noises about leaving, claiming we had no jurisdiction over him, he was on a public street, the whole nine yards. Jacksonville PD keeps a unit nearby for exactly these types of circumstances. I took Trevor Baker in. They took Troy, who was transporting a much more impressive array of drugs."

"And you testified against Troy Baker in court," Aronson confirmed.

"I did. But I think his beef with me may have more to do with the fact I recommended to the Advocate General's Office that Airman Trevor Baker be given time served and a discharge if he testified against his brother as well."

She met Aronson's gaze then his. "Trevor took the deal, but Troy Baker blamed me for his brother's betrayal."

Jake scowled. "How do you know?"

Cass shrugged, then gave him a lopsided smile. "Because he told me as much that day in court."

The colonel gave a short, jerky nod. "There you go." He turned to survey the officers milling around them. "Let me digest this for a minute while I talk to the men."

Cassidy sat with her eyes fixed on something in the distance.

She was clearly deep in thought, no doubt trying to slot all the information and speculation into a narrative that made sense. Bitterness coiled inside him. She didn't deserve this. She hadn't done anything wrong—not then and not now.

"You okay?" He nudged her to rouse her from her reverie.

She startled, then flashed a sheepish little smile as she took the phone back from him. "Yeah, sorry, trying to see if there's any other way to fit the pieces together."

"Seems pretty cut and dried," he reassured her.

Cass nodded quickly and turned her attention back to the screen. "Yeah. Maybe too much." She tapped to open an email. "Oh, good. Bud sent a copy of the rental agreement from the amusement company." She scanned the information. "Class C motorhome. Make, Windward. Model, Enterprise." When her head popped up, she was smiling. "Says here it's black."

Jake turned to survey the lot. The majority of the vehicles parked there were beige, white or silver. When he met her eyes again, he returned the smile. "Excellent."

They watched as the colonel's teams were dispatched to other areas of the grounds. When the older man turned back in their direction, Jake held up his phone. "We have a description of the RV the amusement company rented. We're going to see if we can spot it."

The colonel turned to look out over the sea of parked vehicles. "Locate and report back."

Jake raised a hand to acknowledge the order. Aronson turned to head back up the hill before Cass had even disengaged the parking brake on the cart.

Over the piercing beep of the backup warning, she called to him, "You take the right side. I'll take the left."

They whizzed along the lane, heads turned away from one another as they scanned the packed lot. At last, Jake pointed. "Up ahead on the right."

Cass let off the gas and they rolled to a near-silent stop two spots away from the vehicle. Jake gave Max the signal to stay as he climbed down from the seat. Cass elbowed him sharply, then pointed to the model badge on the driver's side of the hood. A sleek chrome emblem proclaimed it to be an Enterprise.

Cass tipped her head to indicate she'd take a frontal approach. He gestured back, letting her know he'd circle from the rear and meet her at the door on the passenger side.

The coach's dark paint job sparkled in the slanting afternoon sunlight. He noted two good-size bump-outs on the driver's side. A matte-black ladder provided access to the roof from the rear of the vehicle. He placed a foot on the bottom rung and pulled himself up to check it. The vents, A/C unit and what appeared to be a satellite receiver were all camouflaged by the same matte-black finish. Moving slowly to keep from rocking the camper, he lowered himself back to the weedy gravel.

When he came around the corner, he found Cass waiting for him, eyebrows raised. "You wanna kick the tires, too?"

"If I wanted to hide, I'd catch some rays up there," he explained in a harsh whisper.

She shook her head. "He's not hiding. He's gone. And he left the door wide open for us."

Jake frowned and the hairs on the back of his neck rippled. "Wide open?"

She stepped back and made a grand sweeping gesture toward the entrance to the RV. He grasped her arm and gently moved her behind him as he pulled his gun from its holster. "Let me go first."

"The colonel said to report back," she said.

"It's clearly been abandoned."

She rolled her eyes. "Brawn before brains."

He reached back to his academy days for a comeback. "Never backtalk a guy with a Glock."

At the edge of the door, he stopped and took a cautious peek around the edge. Then, leading with his weapon, he called into the camper, "Police! Come out with your hands in the air."

There was no movement within. Glancing over his shoulder, he said, "Let me make sure we're clear."

"Oh, I insist," she said, giving his back a gentle push with her fingertips.

Shaking his head at her ability to maintain her sass under all circumstances, he swung into the open doorway with gun extended. He took a step up into the camper, and Cass turned to press herself against the side.

"There may be a sleeper up front and bedroom in back."

Jake didn't answer. His focus was as locked and loaded as his weapon. He checked the high bunk over the captain's chairs, then made his way to the rear to be sure no one lurked in the bedroom, closet or the tiny toilet.

"We're clear." He jerked his head for Cass to come in but made no move to holster his weapon.

Cass hopped up into the RV and stopped short when she saw the setup inside. The U-shaped dinette area was filled with computer monitors and peripherals. Each of the screens was divided into eight tiles. Each tile provided a live feed to various cameras placed throughout the midway and carnival games. The feed to the monitor on the far right appeared to be frozen.

Cocking his head to the side, Jake realized the camera seemed to be pointed at an angle of what appeared to be asphalt.

"Jake, look," Cass said, sounding breathless as she pointed to a second monitor. Some of the tiles showed security camera footage of the livestock barns. "They're monitoring the barns? They have no equipment set up there," she noted.

He leaned closer, then pointed to one of the squares. "The Swine Barn."

"He's been keeping an eye on all the locations we've identified. And on me." Then she indicated to a third monitor. There, stacked one window atop another, were multiple screenshots of Cassidy seated on the carousel.

Jake hung back as she bent forward to squint at the blurry still shots. He turned in a slow circle, mentally cataloging everything of interest. Discarded boxes from pay-as-you-go mobile phones. Random lengths of wire or possibly fuse cable. A hunk of misshapen C-4 plastic explosive material. Multiple photographs of Cassidy.

Judging by changes in her apparel, Baker must have been watching her for several days at least. He did a quick scan of the kitchenette behind him and spotted a laptop sitting open. He swiped the trackpad with a knuckle, and it sprang to life. A spreadsheet filled with random phone numbers filled the screen. A small window at the bottom right corner prompted him to compose a text message.

"Why would he leave all this?" Cass cast about as if the answer might be lying out in the open with the rest of the evidence. "It's mean. I'm glad he did, but—"

She was reaching for the computer mouse when Max let out three commanding barks.

"Stop," Jake said, grabbing her wrist before she made contact with anything. "It could be rigged," he said almost to himself.

Cass's head jerked up, her eyes wide. "What?"

"It may be rigged to blow," he said, gripping her waist and turning her toward the door. "Otherwise, why would he leave all this? And there's a bomb. We need to get out."

"Wait. How do you—" she protested as he all but shoved her out of the camper.

"Max."

The single word was both a call and an explanation. Holding Cass's hand, he stalked to the front of the RV and saw his partner standing at attention, staring intently on the vehicle's grill.

"Max. Come." He took off in the direction of the entrance

to the lot, breaking into a jog after a few steps, and tugging her along with him.

"Jake—"

He shouted back to her, "We have to get as far away as possible."

"But Max," she huffed, tugging hard on his hand. "He's hurt. Remember?"

Releasing her hand, he whirled to find his partner trying to run on three legs and lagging well behind. "Max," he gasped. He sprinted back to the dog and scooped him into his arms.

"Hang on," she shouted.

He froze in place when Cassidy ran past him. "Don't!" He stood by, watching in horror as she dashed straight back in the direction of the RV.

To his relief, she ran past it and hopped onto the golf cart. Heart pounding in his chest, he cradled Max close as she swung the cart in a wide arc away from the vehicle. Her blond hair blew into her eyes. She pushed it back with the same impatient brush of her hand as he'd seen her use a dozen times throughout the day.

"Look at her." His breath ruffled the dog's fur as she sped to their rescue. "Isn't she great?"

Cassidy jerked to a halt beside them. "Hop on."

He didn't bother with the flatbed. Instead, he dropped heavily into the passenger seat, holding the large dog. "Go."

Cass hit the pedal and the rear tires kicked up gravel as they took off. Craning his neck, he tried to keep the RV in sight as they sped away. Max's breath was hot and stale. The dog let out a disgruntled growl when they hit a bump hard enough to make their teeth clack together.

"Sorry!"

"Keep going." They jolted over uneven ground; he tried to shift Max's girth enough to reach his radio. Cass let up on the accelerator when they approached the gate. "Why are you stopping?"

"Slowing. Hang on." He tightened his grip on the dog as the cart bumped onto the asphalt. She darted a glance at him. "You good?"

"Yeah. All good."

She let off the gas, but did not use the brake, allowing the cart to slow its roll.

Jake pulled the radio from his belt and pressed the button. "Colonel Aronson?" The hum of the cart filled the seconds before the commander's reply came.

"Copy."

"Keep going," he urged Cass, then lifted the radio to his mouth again. "Sir, we have another live one."

"Where?"

"I believe he wired the RV as a trap."

"Return to base," the colonel barked.

"On our way." He turned to Cass and said, "Thirteen."

She nodded, but rather than commenting, she pressed her lips together.

"Baker said a dozen, right?" he reminded her. "He said he planted a dozen explosive devices on the fairgrounds."

She shook her head as they rounded the curve of the arena. "I can't… I don't remember exactly."

He clenched his jaw, hating the shaky self-doubt creeping into her voice. He didn't want her to question her memory or distrust her instincts. She was in this guy's crosshairs precisely because she'd trusted her gut one afternoon long ago, and she had not been wrong. Baker was wrong if he thought he could terrorize her without repercussion.

He didn't need to worry about the full force of the Arkansas State Police coming down on him, though they definitely would. Baker needed to be more concerned about Cassidy Walker snapping out of her shock and setting after him.

"Cass," he said as she let the cart slow to a stop near the arena doors.

She didn't answer him, but stared straight ahead, gripping the wheel so hard her knuckles glowed white.

"Cassidy," he said, injecting a note of command into his voice as he slid Max off his lap to the ground.

"I don't know what he said."

"Cass, we have a record," he reminded her gently. She turned to look at him, a line of puzzlement bisecting her brows. "We have the phone."

She blinked at him, uncomprehending. Then the haze of panic cleared. "The phone?"

"Where is it?"

And almost instantly, the panic was back. "I don't know," she huffed as she groped around on the seat of the golf cart. She squeezed her jacket pockets. Her head whipped around. "It's not here."

"Check your back pocket," he prompted.

Her hands flew to her backside and her shoulders dropped with relief. "Here," she managed to say as she wrestled the device from the pocket of her pants.

But rather than take it from her, Jake caught hold of her arms, prompting her to look up into his eyes. "This is good, Cass. We're safe. Everyone is safe," he said, speaking in a firm tone. "We're safe and we've figured it out because of you. We're going to get him because you figured it out."

"We figured it out."

She looked up into his eyes and, for an instant, he was sixteen and standing on her front porch, gathering the courage to kiss her for the first time. Could he be brave now?

But before he could ponder the possibility a moment longer, Colonel Aronson came through the tinted-glass doors, the team leads from various agencies working the scene following close behind.

"What do you mean 'wired'?" he demanded.

Jake slid off the cart and stood to face the senior officer. "Sir, the door to the recreational vehicle rented by Continental Attractions was left fully ajar. Ms. Walker and I checked the surrounding area, then I checked the interior to be certain no one was inside. It was clear, but he left it as he'd used it. Computer monitors focused on the carousel as well as several of the other sites where explosives were found, even those well off the midway and away from any area the company would have need to monitor."

Aronson pursed his lips as he took it all in. "You think he knew you were closing in on him?"

Jake gave a short nod and crossed his arms over his chest. "I have no doubt. I think the stunt with Agent Parker was an attempt to throw suspicion onto his brother. The fact she went to question the brother at all told him they were on our radar."

"'I've planted explosive devices throughout the fairgrounds,'" Cassidy read, her voice flat.

The crowd turned to look at her, puzzled by the non sequitur, but she was frantically scrolling on the phone as she climbed down from the cart.

"Why did we think it was twelve?"

"What?" Jake moved to her side.

"Why did we assume it was twelve devices?" She looked up then, her searching eyes moving from Jake to the colonel, then to the assembled officers behind him.

"He said twelve, didn't he?" Jake asked.

"He set the first one off at twelve," Evan Furst from the LRFD reminded her.

She nodded distractedly but turned her attention back to the phone. "Oh. Here it is." She tapped the phone screen. "'I've given you a dozen reasons. Cooperate,'" she read, her voice rising with excitement. "He wanted us to think twelve."

Colonel Aronson shot Jake a sidelong glance then said, "Yes, but now we have thirteen."

"Right. Not a dozen-dozen, but a *Baker's dozen*," she announced, as if handing him the key to the whole case on a platter.

Again, the colonel looked to Jake, who shrugged. "She isn't wrong. And this guy is all about the games."

"He thinks he's smarter than everyone," Cass chimed in. "I remember how he was with the Jacksonville police when they came to arrest him, and with the prosecutor, for that matter. He thinks he still has the upper hand, even if we're on to him."

"Apparently, he does," Aronson said.

"I don't think the RV is on a timer, sir." He cleared his throat and forged ahead. "I believe Baker knew we were closing in and he rigged something in the computer setup to be the trigger. If we try to extract anything from there, we could blow all our evidence sky-high."

Aronson turned to the agency leads. "Check in with your teams and see where we are with disabling the other devices."

The order still hung in the air when a woman's voice broke through on the radio. "Cattle Barn 1 is clear, sir."

Aronson reached for his mic. "Confirm successful containment."

"Affirmative, sir. Containment complete," the woman on the other end confirmed.

The assembled group expelled a collective sigh. "Ten-four. Good work."

"Heading over to help at Swine and Sheep," she said. "Sergeant Hinson will deliver the disabled device to base."

The team lead from the LRPD smiled. Hinson and the woman who called the message in were clearly part of his team. He exchanged a speaking glance with the colonel, then pulled out his radio. "You're the best, Loftus. Way to go."

"Thank you, sir," came the brisk reply.

Aronson clapped his hands, drawing their attention back to him. "Okay, we have thirteen devices identified, seven detonated, two disarmed, two out of bounds for now, two in progress." He ran down the list. Turning back to Jake, he said, "What's your read on this guy?"

Jake raised his shoulders in a helpless shrug, then gestured to Cass. "I'm not your best resource, Colonel."

Aronson jerked his chin up in acknowledgment. "No. Of course." He turned to the team leads. "Go check on your people. We're losing daylight, and I want those two deactivated so we can focus on our wildcards."

He turned, surveying the sprawling fairgrounds spread out around them with his hands on his hips while he waited for the others to clear out. When it was the three of them and Max, the colonel slanted his head in the direction of the arena doors. "Come in. This time, we can sit and talk out what we know without worrying about puking our guts up."

Jake turned and gently lifted Max off the bed of the cart. "Speak for yourself, sir. My stomach is still queasy."

He set the dog down and checked to be sure the bandage was still holding. Max fixed him with a bland stare as if to ask if the theatrics were necessary.

Cass turned and ran a hand along the crease of the cart seat before grabbing her balled-up blazer and falling into step behind the colonel. "Where's Bud Thompson?"

"He and a few of the SWAT guys are holding the perimeter around the carousel," Aronson informed her.

"Bud doesn't need to be so close to the bomb," she said worriedly.

"Says the woman who sat with it strapped to her back for hours," Jake said in a laconic drawl. "He knows what he's doing."

"I tried to tell you the same thing, but you seemed to think I had no business doing what I did."

"Yeah, well, that was before I rediscovered what a complete badass you are."

"And don't you forget it," she chided.

Colonel Aronson dropped into a metal folding chair set up behind a collapsible table. He tapped the molded plastic table-top twice to get their attention.

Chapter Seventeen

Cassidy had finished her story about the Baker brothers' arrests when another call came through.

"Picnic area is clear. Confirm deactivation."

Jake smirked and let out a chuckle. "Sounds like Winter's team, sir."

Aronson nodded his understanding. When he turned away to respond to the report, she looked over at Jake. "I can't shake the feeling he's hanging close," she said. "I don't think he cares enough to set off the bomb in the Swine Barn. I think, if anything, the backpack is the one we have to worry about."

"Agreed." He leaned closer. "Assuming I'm correct in believing the RV is rigged and not a remote detonation."

Max's toenails clicked and scraped on the concrete floor as he shifted. Cassidy looked down at the dog who'd become her companion. He twisted around and was nibbling at the gauze wound around his leg to keep the dressing in place.

"Do you think he needs pain meds?"

Jake looked at his K-9, who ceased his exploration the moment he placed a quelling hand on him. "I think he's okay. But if he can't leave it alone, he may get stuck wearing the Cone of Shame."

When the dog's ears twitched and he turned his magnificent nose up, she laughed out loud. "I think he understood you."

"Oh, I have no doubt he did."

Colonel Aronson turned back to them. "The team at the

Swine Barn says they are almost done," he told them. "Leaves us with the backpack and the RV."

"Ms. Walker believes Troy Baker may be somewhere in the area," Jake informed him.

Aronson's attention swung to her. "What makes you think he is?"

Again, she could only answer with a shrug. "Gut feeling? This is a vendetta, Colonel. He's not going to be satisfied until he takes one last shot at me."

Aronson quirked a single brow. "You may be right." Their eyes met and held, his stare challenging, hers telling him she felt up to the task.

"Sir, we can't dangle her out there like bait," Jake argued.

"We can if I say we can," Cassidy countered. When he opened his mouth to argue, she held up a hand. "I appreciate your concern, Jake, but I've been in this up to my neck since the beginning."

"Yeah, but you're out of it now," he countered.

"For how long?" She tilted her head, brows lifting as she waited for his answer. She stood. "Colonel, I'm going to take a walk down to check in on Bud and the rest of the team." She tipped her head toward the door. "You and Max coming with me, or do you prefer to skulk at a distance?"

Jake's expression turned stormy, but before he could retort, the door opened and a silhouetted figure called to them. "Does anyone in here need water? Chief? Sorry I couldn't get back to you, Ms. Walker. My unit needed me."

She squinted against the afternoon glare. The trainee fireman who'd brought her a sandwich earlier stood backlit in the open doorway, but she could read the white print on the snug navy T-shirt he wore. She raised a hand in a wave. "I'm okay, thanks, T.B."

"We're good here," Colonel Aronson said in a clipped tone.

When the door swung shut again, Jake smirked at her. "I think that guy has a crush on you."

Cassidy laughed and rolled her eyes. "Well, of course he does. Look at how pretty I am after being terrorized and held hostage on a runaway merry-go-round."

She rose from the chair and Max scrambled to sit tall. He looked so bright, so alert and ready for action, it was hard to believe he'd been injured. "You don't skulk, do you, big guy?"

"Never," Jake said as he stood, too. "We're sticking with her, sir," he said to Colonel Aronson. A statement, not a request.

"I had no doubt you would."

Cassidy tried to hide her smile as she strode to the doors, confident Jake and Max would be right behind. When they emerged, the sun was close to the horizon, the golden rays of the autumn day morphing into orange and red in their last hurrah. In the shadowy corners of the fairgrounds, lights were coming on. She looked to her right and saw the golf cart was missing.

"We've been cart-jacked."

"It was probably your water boy, gone off to fetch you whatever you might need, Ms. Walker," he mocked.

She snorted. "Keep it up. I haven't seen Jealous Jake since Andy Schmidt asked me to come over to his house so he could copy my biology notes."

Jake scowled and her smile widened. He'd been no slouch back when they were in school, but Andy had been the quarterback and captain of the football team. She'd thought she'd reached a diplomatic solution by getting the secretary to let her run off copies in the school office, but teenage Jake had simmered for a day or two after. He was so cool and contained now, it was hard to imagine him seething over anything.

"I'm not jealous." He looked down at Max, his lips quirking at the corners. "Much."

For his part, Max strained at his shortened lead.

"He looks ready to get back in the action."

Jake nodded but still failed to meet her eyes. "He loves his job."

Deciding she'd let him off the hook—for now—she started down the hill. "Let's let him get back to it."

She'd only gone a few yards when the German shepherd caught up to her, towing Jake behind him. "Hey, no overdoing it, buddy," she admonished, giving him a pat on the neck. "Light duty for you."

They were passing the dairy farms booth when they ran into the team lead for the firefighters.

"Hey," Jake said to the man with "Furst" printed above the emblem on his chest. "How's it going down there?"

"I have a team finishing up in the hog pens." He nodded to Cassidy. "Talked to your guy a couple minutes ago. He had nothing suspicious to report."

"Thank you." Then, remembering the golf cart, she said, "Hey, I think your trainee took off with my cart."

Furst looked puzzled. "Trainee?"

"Yeah. He's been checking on me all afternoon," she told him, hoping to jog his memory. "If you see him, would you tell him to bring the cart down to where Bud and the other guys on surveillance are set up?"

"Uh-huh," Furst said with a vague nod. As they started to move past them, he reached out and snagged her arm. "Wait. We don't have any trainees on site."

"What?" She blinked, confused by both his assertion and his firm grip.

"We don't bring trainees out on calls like this," he said, his voice growing strident. Jake shot a pointed look at the man's hand and the firefighter instantly released her, holding his hand high as if swearing an oath. "Sorry, ma'am."

Cassidy could not have cared less about the man's hand. Her brain was pinging. She glanced at Jake then back to Furst. "There's a guy here wearing a navy-blue shirt with the word

'Trainee' printed below the LRFD. He's been checking in on me regularly." She paused. "Had a hat like yours." She pointed to the cap Furst wore.

Furst tilted his head. "Our trainees don't have special shirts. They wear standard issue. We have them wear vests when we're running a drill but…" He shook his head. It was clear from his expression he knew no such person existed.

Whirling, she pinned Jake with a stare. "You saw him, right?"

Jake nodded. "Earlier, and again a few minutes ago," he confirmed. "What did you call him?"

Everything slowed inside her, sound and light blurring and slurring in the moment before the last piece of the puzzle fell into place. "T.B.," she murmured. "He said everyone called him T.B. Troy—"

"Baker," she and Jake said at the same time.

"Now we know how he always knew what was going on."

"He was walking right up to me all day," she said, incredulous. "He's been toying with us the whole time."

Jake grabbed her hand. She wasn't sure if he was trying to calm her or to keep her from running off to look for Baker. Either way, it was effective.

"Would you catch Colonel Aronson up?" Jake asked Furst, hooking a thumb toward the arena. "I'm betting Baker has a radio, so I don't want to broadcast it. He's seen Cassidy and knows she's still on the case, so I think it's safe to assume he's around here somewhere."

Furst nodded. "I'll take care of it."

Cassidy stood rooted to the spot as they watched the other man jog up the hill. "All day. Right there."

"We knew he had eyes on you. And ears, I guess."

Flexing her jaw, she drew a deep breath and set out for the midway. She didn't have to break stride for Jake and Max to catch up to her easily.

"What are you planning to do?" Jake huffed.

"We're going to draw him out."

"We need a plan."

"Plans haven't gotten us anywhere," she snapped. "We've been making up plans and pulling threads all day." She stopped, throwing her arms out wide. "It's all unraveled now, Jake. We don't have time to think and plan. It's going to get dark soon, and the minute it does, everything shifts even more to his advantage. We need to act. The sun is going down and so is this jerk."

Without waiting for him to reply, she set out on a trajectory straight for the crumpled carousel. The wreckage of the Ferris wheel cast creepy, elongated shadows on the pavement. The glitter-and-gilt-painted horses beneath the crushed canopy were not only garish, but a little ghoulish as well.

"Looks like the set of a horror film," she said.

"Don't even," Jake growled. "Cass, I can't let you go off half-cocked like this—"

"You're not letting me," she shot back. "And I'm not half-cocked. I'm locked and loaded. I'm telling you I'm over this." She made a chopping motion with her hand, then cast a wary glance at the carousel where she'd been held captive for hours. "It needs to stop. I'm getting off this ride."

She looked back at him, but rather than glaring down at her with his familiar scowl set in stone, he was staring off at a spot south of the mangled amusements.

"What?"

Whirling to follow the line of his stare, she froze when she saw what had captured his attention. There, parked alongside the Mystery Maze Fun House, sat the golf cart they'd left outside the arena.

The one Troy Baker had likely commandeered.

She started in direction, but Jake caught her again. "No. Wait."

"I'm not waiting," she growled.

"Let Max check it first," he said through gritted teeth. "We've seen what he's capable of doing," he reminded her with a sweeping gesture toward the mass of mangled steel and wood. He spoke slowly and firmly. "Let Max do his job."

"Fine," she agreed. "But I'm sticking with you."

"I wouldn't have it any other way." He let his hand slide down to grasp hers, and together they made a beeline for the cart.

Stopping a few yards back, Jake let go of her hand only long enough to free Max from his lead. He reclaimed her hand again, and she squeezed his as they watched the dog circle the vehicle, giving it wide berth at first, then moving in for a closer inspection.

"He's not finding anything."

"How do you know?"

"He gives signals. If he was picking up anything, he would have pointed by now."

"Pointed?"

"That big schnozz isn't for show. Not only can he separate and identify hundreds of scents, but he also uses it as a traffic baton. He points, gestures with it, uses it to dig, if necessary. It's a multipurpose tool."

She watched as Max circled the cart again and then hopped up into the front seat to give it a good sniff. Eventually, he sat and turned to look in their direction, tongue hanging out the side of his mouth.

Jake tugged her forward. "Come on. It's clear."

"You trust him that much?"

"I trust him implicitly," Jake answered without a hint of hesitation. "If Max says it's safe, it's safe."

When they reached the cart, Jake had a treat in hand. "Good boy."

Cassidy turned in a slow circle, taking in the area around them. Then she spotted something dark lying on the metal ramp leading to the Fun House entrance. She took two steps in that direction, her hand sliding from Jake's grip as she squinted at the object.

"Oh, it's a hat," she said, a nervous laugh bubbling out of her.

"What?" Jake turned and peered in the direction she indicated.

"There's a hat on the ramp," she explained. Tilting her head to the side, she saw there was white printing on the crown. Her breath caught in her throat, and she whirled back to him, her eyes wide. "It's a LRFD hat."

"Hang on." He snapped his fingers and pointed to the ground. Max hopped down from the cart, head lifted and ears pricked with anticipation. "Go get it," Jake said, pointing to the hat.

Max fetched and delivered the hat into Jake's hand without a beat of hesitation. Jake pinched the brim of the hat and turned it over to inspect it. "Baker was wearing a hat?"

Cassidy nodded, recalling how she'd thought the man was using the curled brim to shield his eyes from the glaring sun. "Yes. He kept it pulled down."

"This hat?" He turned it so she could see the front.

"Or one like it," she confirmed.

He nodded once, then lowered it so Max could give the inside a good sniff. "It was a warm day. I'm sure Baker worked up a sweat." Then he knelt down to speak to his partner. "Got it?"

Max slow-blinked, as if Jake had asked a silly question.

Smirking, Jake straightened then gestured to the ramp. "Go find him."

The dog took off at a gallop. His toenails clicked and skittered on the metal ramp. He sped to the top then ducked through a curtain made of wide strips of black vinyl.

Jake and Cass followed him into attraction, stumbling into one another as they tried to get their footing on a floor tilted at a sharp enough angle to send them careening into walls.

"It would be the Fun House," Cass grumbled as they made it to the other end.

Before Jake could answer, they fell into the next room. It was completely inflatable. A bounce-house with inflated flooring, walls and furniture. They bounced around a bit before Jake finally dropped to his side and rolled toward the exit. Cass quickly followed suit.

Breathless and sweating, they tumbled into the next room – a square of dark walls covered in neon paint graffiti lit by black lights. It was so dark, Jake hadn't realized the flooring had been replaced by industrial rollers until he landed on his backside.

Cass helped him to his feet. "That can't be safety approved," he muttered as he found his footing.

"A lawsuit waiting to happen," Cass concurred.

"Of course, they'll be out of town before anything could happen, and I doubt they run cameras in here."

At the end of the roller walkway, Jake peeked around the doorframe to get a glimpse of their next obstacle. A room covered in mirrors from floor to ceiling. There was even an enormous mirrored ball dangling from the ceiling.

The room was unlit, but enough of an opening in the rear access panels for daylight to seep in. They stepped into room only to find the walls were angled to reflect back on themselves.

Cassidy groaned. "The last thing I needed right now was a look in the mirror."

Jake chuckled, but he was too busy scanning the floor for obstacles to take a peek at himself. He was about to assure her she looked fine to him when the lights came on and the Fun House sprang to life.

They instinctively raised their hands to shield their eyes from the glare, but it was the noise made his heart start racing. Rock music blared over the squeal of metal gears meshing and the amped up hum of a generator.

The mirror ball sent hundreds of spots bouncing endlessly off the walls, the floor and the ceiling.

Cassidy had just lowered her arm when they heard someone call from the next room, "Having fun, Lieutenant?"

"It's him," she whispered, her gaze transfixed on a point in the center of the room.

"I left you a present, Lieutenant," the man shouted over the cacophony of sound. "Why don't you try it on again?"

Jake's head whipped around. "Baker? We're onto you, Baker," he called, then started in the direction of the voice. He'd gone two steps before he caught sight of what held her attention.

The backpack.

Baker had left the backpack directly under the faceted ball. Without a moment of hesitation, Jake grabbed Cass's wrist and pulled her toward the exit to the next room.

"Bomb," she panted, stumbling to keep up.

"He's in here. He won't detonate it until he's clear," Jake shouted back.

The next room featured a floor made of alternating metal platforms seesawing at varied rates and a giant black-and-white painted spiral undulating at the far end. He was about to jump onto the first plank when he spotted an open-grate catwalk running along the back of the room.

He changed directions so suddenly Cass let out a yelp. "Sorry. Looks like mechanical access," he explained as he led her to the blessedly stationary walkway.

The catwalk was only about a foot wide, so they had to scuttle along it side-by-side. Still, it was faster than trying to navigate the obstacles.

"Baker?" Jake shouted the man's name. It was both a test and a warning. But no reply came. "We have to get out of here fast," he said, speaking low enough for only Cass to hear.

"There should be exit panels back here," she answered, panting. "They have to be able to take patrons who get overwhelmed out fast."

Sure enough, just up ahead, Jake spotted a wooden door painted black with a green light shining above it. He stiff-armed it the moment they were within reach, but it was the force of a blast that sent them sprawling out onto the asphalt.

Jake rolled toward Cass. "Are you all right?"

"I'm okay. I'm okay," she said grimacing as she brushed her hands over the front of her pants.

There was a moment of eerie silence as music and machinery cut out. They scooted away from the structure, taking refuge behind one of the trailers used to haul the disassembled rides. They watched in stunned silence as the Fun House crumbled in on itself, smoke rising from the center.

Jake looked around. There didn't seem to be anyone at the rear of the midway. Everyone was out front, getting ready to race into chaos. Everyone except Baker. But Jake had no doubt he was still nearby. Still watching to see if he'd gotten the job done.

He was startled from his thought when Max let out three sharp barks.

"That's Max," she said.

Jake hadn't needed her confirmation, but the fact that she knew Max's bark well enough to identify him made something warm blossom in his chest.

"It's a warning."

"Think he's spotted Baker?" Cass asked as they scrambled to their feet.

"Baker or another bomb." He checked in both directions, then pointed toward the wreckage of the carousel and Ferris wheel. "Let's go this way. I don't want him to see us if we can help it."

They almost made it to the other end of the Fun House when they saw a figure dressed in dark clothes jump onto the tilted platform and duck down between the horses.

"Baker." Cass exhaled.

A second later, Max jumped onto the carousel as well, his target in his sights.

"He's got him pinned down," she shouted over her shoulder.

They drew up at the undamaged side of the carousel and looked around. Max was nowhere to be seen. But then they heard him.

He gave only two barks this time, but the relieved smile spreading across Jake's face screamed, "Jackpot!'"

"What? What is it?"

"He found what we're looking for." Jake was unable to contain his grin.

He pulled his radio free as they ran toward the carousel. When they arrived, they found Max sitting on top of someone sprawled between the seahorse benches, his gleaming teeth bared.

"Hold, Max." Then he spoke into the radio. "Trooper Jake Donovan. Suspect apprehended by K-9 Trooper Max on the carousel, currently held between the green benches on the southeast side. Requesting assistance and transport."

"Get him off me!" Baker bellowed.

"Not a chance," Jake replied.

Then, before he could stop her, Cassidy pushed past him to squat down at look Baker in the face. "Once again, I'm going to miss out on the fun of being the one who gets to arrest you, Troy." The other man blinked, then snarled, hurling an unsavory epitaph at her as she straightened. But Cass simply smiled. "Don't worry. I'll see you again soon, Mr. Baker. In court."

In the blink of an eye, they were swarmed by the security and SWAT officers who'd been guarding the perimeter. But Max held his ground with the suspect, growling and baring his impressive teeth.

"How'd he make it past us?" Bud Thompson huffed as he drew to a halt beside Cassidy.

She held up the hat with the fire department logo. "He's been posing as a firefighter. Been running all over the place all day."

Officers from the SWAT team moved in, and Jake gave the command for Max to back down. The moment Baker was cuffed, Jake whistled and Max bounded down from the platform, clearly pleased with his day's work.

"Hey, do we need to..." She hooked a thumb in the direction of the Fun House. "Was there something in there?"

Cassidy hung back, Jake sticking close to her side. "I guess we were wrong in thinking we were dealing in dozens, baker's or otherwise."

"It was as good a guess as any," Jake said. He didn't look at her as the police escorted Baker off the ride.

A part of her wanted to confront him. To crow about his failures and revel in her escape. But the officers who took him into custody led him away in the direction of the north gate where a number of cruisers sat parked along Roosevelt Road.

"Sarge?" One of the firefighters checking the area around the bench raised an arm. Evan Furst stepped up to the edge of the platform and the man handed something down to him.

Cassidy watched as he bagged the object as evidence, conferred with Colonel Aronson, then handed the bag over. A few minutes later, Sergeant Furst made his way over to them.

"We have his phone," the firefighter said as he approached. "Your team will take a closer look, but it looks like he was using the device for remote detonation." He shrugged. "Not uncommon when dealing with IEDs."

Cassidy frowned. "I don't ever want to use a mobile phone again."

Both men laughed. "Try to order pizza without one," Jake said, rolling his eyes.

Furst slapped Jake on the back, then offered his knuckles to Max for a sniff. "Your boy here put quite the scare into our guy." As if on cue, Max smiled up at him, his giant pink tongue unfurling like a banner trailing out the side of his mouth.

"Yes, he can look scary when he wants to," Jake said, giving the dog an affectionate pat.

Sergeant Furst offered his hand to her. "You were something, Ms. Walker. I don't know many people who could have hung in there like you did."

She accepted the handshake with a tired smile. "I have the constitution of a twelve-year-old."

Furst chuckled then stepped aside as Colonel Aronson approached. "Ms. Walker, I have to ask you for your phone," the older man said, cushioning the request with a note of apology.

"Of course," Cassidy said. She reached into her back pockets and extracted a phone from each. "I was telling Agent Donovan I didn't think I'd be using my phone much anymore."

The older man gave an appreciative huff, then frowned at the two devices she offered. "Did the suspect contact you on both devices?"

"No, sir." She raised her right hand slightly higher. "His messages came through on this one. My personal line."

Aronson took the proffered phone. "Hate to make a long day even longer, but would you mind coming to headquarters to make your statement?"

Cassidy nodded. "No problem."

He ran a hand over his buzz-cut hair. "He had no ID on him, but his prints will be in the system, so it shouldn't be an issue."

He nodded to the phone in her other hand. "I'll leave the other with you. Unless there's evidence linked directly to our perp, we won't need it."

"Oh. Okay." She tucked the phone Bud had provided for her back into her pocket. "I suppose I'm gonna need it. We're going to be scrambling to get this cleaned up and get things going."

The colonel nodded. "In case you haven't heard, the governor's office has already announced a three-day delay on the opening."

Her brows shot up with surprise. "Wow. Three days. Okay. I guess we have our work cut out for us."

"Maybe Ms. Walker could come in to give her statement in the morning?" Jake suggested. "It's been one heck of a day, sir."

But Cassidy shook him off. "No. Tonight would be better for me. I'm going to have a million things to do before we can open." She turned to look at Jake. "You go on. I'll be along as soon as I can."

"I can keep an eye on things," Bud Thompson interrupted. "They're going to be processing the scene for hours, if not a day or two." He jerked his chin in Cassidy's direction. "You get out of here for a bit. You'll have to hit the ground running once they give us the go-ahead to clean up."

She whirled to ask Colonel Aronson if he thought it would actually take days, but the man was gone. She spotted him walking toward the south lot with one of the police captains. "Days?"

Bud shrugged. "Let's see how things play out. I'll hang around."

Cassidy pressed the tips of her fingers to the center of her forehead, then rubbed in tiny circles, working to her temples. "Days," she whispered.

Jake leaned in as Bud walked away. "Don't worry about that yet."

He placed a hand on her back, and for the first time since he'd hopped onto her merry-go-round this morning, Cassidy didn't feel duty-bound to pull away.

"The governor's office had to give the press something," he continued in a soothing tone. "No one expects you to—"

He stopped talking abruptly as she turned into him, burying her face in the base of his throat. His arms came around her and she sank deep into his embrace. Lips moving against the fabric of his shirt, she mumbled, "It started out such a good day."

She felt rather than heard his chuckle. "I don't know," he crooned into her hair. "It's not ending too badly."

Pulling back, she tipped her chin up to look into his eyes. "You think?"

"I know." Lowering his mouth to hers, he kissed her sweetly. When they parted, he pressed his forehead to hers. "Hey, Cass?"

"Yeah?"

"I'm gonna need a date for the fair."

She chuckled as she allowed herself to be tucked back into his embrace. "Well, what do you know? It so happens I'll be here every day."

Epilogue

Cassidy stood at the top of the hill looking down at the crowded midway. If anyone had asked her a day ago if they'd ever get the fair up and running, she would have been torn between laughter and tears. But here they were, open for business and welcoming record-setting crowds.

As Colonel Aronson had predicted, Troy Baker's identity had been confirmed before she'd even left State Police headquarters the night of his arrest. He'd continued to play cat and mouse with the investigators well into the next day, but eventually they'd informed him they were sitting on a pile of evidence high enough for them to move ahead with or without his statement.

Then Baker's tale of woe and persecution came tumbling out.

For her part, Cassidy had spent the past few days trying to focus on the task at hand. A conversation with Trevor Baker went a long way in helping her understand his convoluted reasoning. Troy Baker believed she turned his brother against him, and if they hadn't both testified in court, he would have received a lighter sentence. And he might still have a relationship with his brother.

Cassidy knew there was nothing she could do to set their relationship to rights, but she could focus on getting the grounds cleared and secured. The governor's office, the board of directors and the fair's staff had done most of the hustling.

Once the damaged rides were removed from the site, a local amusement company had brought in an elaborate inflatable obstacle course to fill open spaces. From the length of the line to go through the course, it looked like the addition was going to be a hit with fairgoers of all ages.

A few of the musical acts set to perform were unable to reschedule and a couple had dropped out, but the entertainment chair was the type of woman who always had backups for her backups, so they were able to make sure the main stage was fully covered.

The livestock judging had resumed early morning, as had the arts, crafts and culinary contests. So far, the revised schedule seemed to be working smoothly. Hands on her hips, she smiled as she pivoted in a semicircle, taking it all in.

"You're looking smug this morning," Jake Donovan said, his voice gruff in her ear.

She didn't jump, or even blink in surprise when his arm slid around her waist. Over the past few days, Jake and Max had quickly melded into the fabric of her life. Letting her head fall back against his shoulder, she hummed noncommittally. "Do I? Good, because I feel smug." She gestured to the festivities. "Can you believe this is happening?"

"I never doubted you for a minute." He tilted his head to brush a kiss to her temple. "Shall we go survey your domain?"

She laughed as she wriggled from his grasp. "We shall."

"Hey, big guy," she cooed, bending down to offer her knuckles to Max. He bathed them with a sloppy kiss. "Thank you. I needed a big sloppy kiss."

"Oh, if that's the case—"

Jake attempted to tug her back into his arms, but she resisted.

"Hey, come on," she said, pushing him away. "Don't be jealous." She took his hand and pulled him in the direction of the midway. "Come on. I'll let you win me an enormous stuffed gorilla."

"You greatly overestimate my basketball skills."

"We'll stick to firing corks at empty cans then," she assured him. "Surely they taught you to shoot at the police academy, didn't they?"

"We need to change the saying to 'Don't mock a man with a Glock.'"

She threw her head back and laughed. Stepping onto the paved lane, they hooked a sharp right, sticking to the arcade side of the midway rather than getting snarled up in the lines queueing for the rides. As they passed the corn dog stand, Cassidy waved to Manny, who was busy working the deep fryer.

They paused to watch a couple of teenagers taking their best shots at the basketball hoops. They were so engrossed in the competition between a young man and woman, they barely noticed Manny's approach.

But Max did.

The dog let out a woof of approval as he eyed the footlong corn dogs the older man offered like a prized bouquet.

"Oh! Thank you, Manny," she said, beaming at her friend.

"Thank you," Jake said as he took one of the proffered treats.

"The least I can do," Manny said, pulling packets of mustard from an apron pocket. "And if I may, I have something for our hero," he said, raising expectant brows at Jake as he gestured to Max.

"Oh, I'm sorry. He eats a specialized diet—"

Manny pulled a paper-wrapped package from the same pocket and presented it to Jake. "Miss Cassidy told me he had to be treated special. I have a little chicken for him. Not much. No seasonings. Good chicken."

He looked so hopeful. Cassidy held her breath as she, Manny and poor salivating Max awaited his answer.

Jake looked from Manny to her, then back again. "Oh. That's very nice of you. Thank you." He accepted the gift on Max's behalf.

"You're sweet, Manny," Cassidy said, leaning in to hug him.

"Now, get back to it before we have a corn dog revolt on our hands."

Manny waved and flashed a bright smile as he backed away. He took three steps then turned and took off for his battered food stand at a dead run, expertly dodging meandering fairgoers as they stepped into his path.

She nodded toward a bench only half occupied by a woman rocking a stroller to and fro. "Let's settle for a minute."

It wasn't until she took a seat on the bench that she realized she was staring straight at the spot where the carousel stood. "Oh."

He frowned down at her. "You wanna move?"

"No. No." She waved his concern away. "I'm good." She plucked the corn dog from his hand. "Here, I'll hold this while you take care of Max."

"Okay." He chuckled as he unwrapped the package. When he saw the palm-size pile of boneless, skinless chicken, he smiled. "This was nice of him. Max will generally behave himself, but he is a dog, after all."

"As evidenced by the drooling," she said, nodding to the slobber trickling from the corners of the dog's mouth.

Sure enough, Max gulped down the offering in record time. Satisfied with his treat, he stretched out at Cassidy's feet and took in the crowd passing by.

After relinquishing Jake's treat, Cassidy squeezed a thin line of mustard along the cornbread-battered hot dog and took a hearty bite. "I still can't believe you showed up here," she said, talking through stuffed cheeks.

Jake was polite enough to wait until he'd swallowed his bite to respond. "The minute I realized the woman slipping a backpack containing heaven knows what onto her back was you, I almost lost it."

"Yeah, well, if you think you're going to dump me after this trip to the fair, I'd think again," she warned, pointing the corn dog at him. "I'm not as sweet as I used to be."

"Yes, you are." Jake exhaled loudly, turning to look at the spot where they'd met again after so many years. "Thankfully, I'm not as dumb as I used to be."

"So, we have that going for us," she said, flashing a cheeky smile.

But Jake remained somber. "You know it wasn't you, right?"

"What?"

"It's a cliché, I know. But aren't all teenagers?"

He tilted his head in the direction of the free-throw game, where the couple who'd been competing minutes before were now kissing.

"I was so in love with you, I didn't know what to do. I convinced myself you didn't feel the same way about me, so I thought it would be better if I..."

"Dumped me?" she interjected.

"Saved myself," he argued.

"And now you've saved me." She flashed him a rueful smile. "You're quite the heroes, you and Max."

"I could do the whole bit about doing my job, ma'am, but I think we both know this was different." His smile was crooked, but it felt as warm as the bright sunshine. "I guess I should say different and still the same."

"How?"

"Different because we're not kids anymore," he said.

He looked down at her, searching her eyes as if they might hold all the answers. But all she had for him was a spill of sentimental tears.

She reached up to touch his cheek. "And still the same?"

"Because I saw you and all I could think was how much I still love you."

She exhaled in a whoosh and the woman on the bench next

to her gave a soft, "Oooooh," as she jumped up. "Here you go. Sit here."

"Wait—" Jake protested.

But the woman already had her phone pressed to her ear. "Oh my gosh, I heard the sweetest thing," she crowed, nudging the stroller ahead of her. They were quickly swallowed up by the crowd.

Cassidy beamed as Jake took the seat the woman vacated. "It was the sweetest thing," she said, wrinkling her nose playfully. "We may need to book dentist appointments."

"Not right now," he said, leaning in to steal a soft kiss from her.

She angled her head, inviting him to make the kiss last a little longer.

He accepted.

When they finally pulled back, Cass was wearing her heart in her eyes, but she didn't have the energy or the inclination to shield herself. Not after all they'd been through. Not after all the years they'd wasted.

"I still love you, too."

Jake smiled and started to move in for another kiss, but suddenly someone yanked her corn dog straight out of her hand.

"What the—" she started, then stopped when she spotted Max holding the mustard-smeared remains between his paws and cheerfully gnawing it off the stick.

"Not so well-trained after all," she said.

"Corn dogs are not his area of expertise." Jake shrugged, then offered the remainder of his corn dog to his partner. "It's okay. I have a feeling we're going to need to be hands free for a while."

With that, he slid his fingers into her hair and planted one on her as if there was a blue ribbon in kissing on the line.

* * * * *

Don't miss the next installment of
Arkansas Special Agents
by Maggie Wells,
On sale September 2026,
Wherever Harlequin books and ebooks are sold!

Get up to 4 Free Books!

**We'll send you 2 free books from each series you try
PLUS a free Mystery Gift.**

Both the **Harlequin Intrigue®** and **Harlequin® Romantic Suspense** series feature compelling novels filled with heart-racing action-packed romance that will keep you on the edge of your seat.

YES! Please send me 2 FREE novels from the Harlequin Intrigue or Harlequin Romantic Suspense series and my FREE gift (gift is worth about $10 retail). I may cancel anytime by emailing ReaderServiceInfo@Harlequin.com or by calling 1-800-873-8635. If I don't cancel, I will receive 6 brand-new Harlequin Intrigue Larger-Print books every month and be billed just $7.19 each in the U.S. or $7.99 each in Canada, or 4 brand-new Harlequin Romantic Suspense books every month and be billed just $6.39 each in the U.S. or $7.19 each in Canada, a savings of 20% off the cover price. It's quite a bargain! Shipping and handling is just 75¢ per book in the U.S. and $1.75 per book in Canada.* I understand that accepting the free books and gift places me under no obligation to buy anything—they are mine to keep for free no matter what I decide.

Choose one:

☐ **Harlequin Intrigue Larger-Print**
(199/399 BPA G3CD)

☐ **Harlequin Romantic Suspense**
(240/340 BPA G3CD)

☐ **Or Try Both!**
(199/399 & 240/340 BPA G3CE)

Name (please print)

Address   Apt. #

City   State/Province   Zip/Postal Code

Email: Please check this box ☐ if you would like to receive newsletters and promotional emails from Harlequin Enterprises ULC and its affiliates. You can unsubscribe anytime.

Mail to the **Harlequin Reader Service:**
IN U.S.A.: P.O. Box 1341, Buffalo, NY 14240-8531
IN CANADA: P.O. Box 603, Fort Erie, Ontario L2A 5X3

Want to explore our other series or interested in ebooks? **Visit www.ReaderService.com or call 1-800-873-8635.**

HIHRS2603